FOREWORD

If I thought the author of the Cobb Mountain Mystery Series was brilliant before, after reading the conclusion of the series, I am convinced of her genius.

DeCanti's ability to lead us into and out of situations goes beyond mere story-telling. Her descriptive words convince us we're there. We see with our mind's eye the places and people she introduces us to. We love, we hate, we cry, and yes, we *suspect* characters we once loved as questions we didn't know we had about the five previous books in the series are brought forth, astounding us with the answers.

I'm saddened, as I'm sure are you, to know this will be our last adventure on Cobb Mountain. I'm just as sure we will all revisit the Cobb Mountain Mystery Series often.–Valeri Neff, Hope Blend Foundation

Who doesn't like a good mystery? How about one that begins in Ireland, crosses the Atlantic in a majestic sailing vessel, then continues westward on at least one wagon train and finally plays out a few generations later in one of the most beautiful places in the world, Lake County, California? How about a mystery that takes five books to tell?

Each book complete on its own, or so we think, until questions start to rear their nasty little heads. Then Miss Kit answers them in her final book! And now, the series finished, we are left wondering no more. Satisfied, but disappointed the journey is over, I guess I'll go back and read the first book again.

~Susan Little–Boyle, Mississippi

STOP RIGHT NOW if you haven't already read the first 5 books in the series—you are robbing yourself of the full enjoyment of 'series.' Plus, there will be people, places, and events you will not understand. Although I hate to see it end, I've never enjoyed a mystery series as much in my life. ~Charlie Raincrow–Valley Springs, CA

Journey To Cobb Mountain–Beginnings took us on a ride that led us, head and heart first, over a cliffhanger the magnitude of which the only recovery is this much-awaited finale to this brilliant mystery series.
~Dr. Robert Gardner–Lucerne, CA,

The last book left us to wonder about the future of The Fumaroles and Kat and Little Jimmy, the last we heard of them they were in the tunnel of Kat's nightmares! I couldn't rest until I knew the answers to these dilemmas. Again, we are not disappointed as Kit DeCanti's relentless effort to terrorize has yet again proved successful.

~Marti Brown–Santa Cruz, CA, U.S.A.

Every book in Kit DeCanti's Cobb Mountain Series took us on an adventure of suspense, and mystery leading us to this final book: Cobb Mountain–Journey's End. In our travels around beautiful Lake County, all the characters came to the end of their journey, in many ways, taking us by surprise! Another masterpiece by Kit DeCanti, one of my favorite authors.

~Margie Lowery–Bella Vista, CA, U.S.A.

Kit DeCanti's Books

THE COBB MOUNTAIN MYSTERY SERIES, in this order:
SECRET ON COBB MOUNTAIN (released 2009)
RETURN TO COBB MOUNTAIN (released 2010)
KONOCTI CAVES (released 2011)
CROSSROADS INN TIME (released 2012)
JOURNEY TO COBB MOUNTAIN—Beginnings (released 2018)
COBB MOUNTAIN—Journey's End (released 2023)

Additional works by Kit DeCanti

SECRET OF A LAZY COOK—Or How I Survived Marriage to
an Italian When I Hate the Kitchen

Available at

htpp://www.decantiproductions.com

and your local bookstores

Published by DeCanti Productions

Most books by Kit DeCanti are available at special

quantity discounts for bulk purchases

or sales promotions, premiums or fund raising.

Special books or book excerpts can also be created to fit

specific needs by publisher, only with prior permission from author.

FOR DETAILS contact Editor: editor@decantiproductions.com

COBB MOUNTAIN–JOURNEY'S END

by

Kit DeCanti

Published by DeCanti Productions

>^..^<

First printing: April 2023

Printed in the U.S.A.

Published by DECANTI PRODUCTIONS

ISBN: 9798378333011

Imprint: Independently published

So many to thank, as I bring my Cobb Mountain Mystery Series to a close. Where to begin?

First, I want to give special thanks to all my faithful and patient readers, who prodded and pushed me to get the second, third, fourth, and fifth books in the Cobb Mountain Mystery Series finished—which led to this last book. Without all your threats, it would have never happened. Thank you all who pushed, *not so patiently,* for this sequel to Secret on Cobb Mountain, Return to Cobb Mountain, Konocti Caves, Crossroads Inn Time, Journey to Cobb Mountain–Beginnings. So, dear friends, now with so many mixed emotions and separation anxiety, I present: Cobb Mountain–Journey's End. Thanks to each and every one of you.

To all my friends and family who have believed in me, encouraged me, and suffered through the insanity all writers experience as we live in these dual dimensions—the 'here and now' while writing in the 'there and then.'

And to my Mom, who loved to tell stories of her youth, growing up in rural Missouri and vacationing at her grandparents' large plantation home in Arkansas. And my favorite story of how she met my dad. The historical parts of Journey to Cobb Mountain are loosely—very loosely—based on Mom's stories, which were loosely—very loosely—based on facts, that changed a little with each telling. I miss her stories, and wish I could listen to them another dozen or more times, and see the smile that caused her cute nose to wrinkle as she spoke of her childhood, her Dad and her Grandpa Sam Spears, and how she met Daddy. Her family stories and histories inspired the last two books of this series, and me to start writing in the first place. Mom, I haven't forgotten my promise of a book based on your stories. I love and miss you.

And what can I say to the genius who helped me get this book together and ready for edit? My dearest and longtime friend, Sue Little, who up and moved from California to Mississippi to become the Southern Belle she was meant to be; and who, in preparation of this book, tirelessly reread my books to make sure they all jived. Or as she would say having given up her California slang for a proper southern twang, "jahved". Sue's brilliance is only outdone by her modesty. I thank you, SuzieQ, for lending your talent to prep this, my final book. But mostly, thank you for being my loyal friend and confidant for 37 years! And Ramona Scruggs whom I've loved since she was a teenybopper. Who knew you were going to grow up to be such a great proofreader! Love you 'little girl!'

And there is so much I need to say in thanks to my 'Editor and Chief' not to mention dear friend, and Word Nerd extraordinaire, Valarie Allinder, for her never-ending encouragement, kindness and patience, while eagerly waiting to get her *ruthlessly infamous and feared red pen* on Cobb Mountain– Journey's End. All kidding aside Valarie, you saved my books. Thank you!

And last but not least, how can I ever find words to thank my BIGGEST fan: my husband and soulmate, Tony, who has been with me for every step, fall, and twist of this roller coaster 'journey.' He's been next to me, cheering me on, from the first night I read a passage from my Secret on Cobb Mountain, until I struck the last key in Journey's

End. He's supported me and has been, though perhaps not perfectly, patient with me, more patient than one would think humanly possible as I wandered through the dual dimension of my Cobb Mountain world for the past 10+ years, speaking of people whose identities he learned in order to keep up with my insanity, never judging my emotional explosions and who never stopped loving me. And in whose eye I detected a tear as I read the last line of my beloved Cobb Mountain Mystery Series. Thank you for always reminding me that the hero has to get the girl. You're my hero and I'll always be your girl! I love you Captain, O' My Captain. It has been quite a journey. But ours is far from over.

AS THIS BOOK GOES TO PRESS SADLY SOME BUSINESSES LISTED BELOW HAVE NOT SURVIVED THE RECENT YEARS OF WILDFIRES THAT RAVAGED BEAUTIFUL LAKE COUNTY, OR THE COVID PANDEMIC. I WANT TO SAY THANK YOU TO THE FOLLOWING BUSINESSES AND LOCATIONS FOR ALLOWING ME THE PRIVILEGE OF USING THEIR NAMES IN THE CONTENT OF THIS BOOK AND MAY THIS BOOK SERVE AS A MEMORIAL FOR THE YEARS OF SERVICE TO OUR COMMUNITY:

Children's Museum of Art and Science (CMAS) ~ Lake Co, CA

Riviera Common Grounds Coffee House ~ Kelseyville, CA

Little House Family Day Care~ Clearlake, CA

Boar's Breath Smokin' BBQ ~ Clearlake, CA

Main Street Bar and Grill ~ Clearlake, CA

Mountain High Coffee & Books ~ Cobb, CA

Clearlake Cinema~ Clearlake, CA

Black Rock Golf Course ~ Cobb, CA

Cactus Grill Restaurant ~ Clearlake, CA

Heidi's Hair Care ~ Santa Rosa, CA

Park Place Restaurant ~ Lakeport, CA

School House Museum ~ Lower Lake, CA

Shannon Ridge Winery ~ Clearlake Oaks, CA

Taylor Observatory, Norton Planetarium ~ Kelseyville, CAs

Record Bee ~ Lakeport, CA

Hardester's Market ~ Cobb, CA

Cobb Mountain Pizza ~ Cobb, CA

Saw Shop ~ Kelseyville, CA

Dedicated to my daughter,

Angela Kay DeCanti Woodall

for your loyalty, love, and all the

joy you have given me.

I've always written for

and to you.

I love you.

PROLOG

By the time Kat Simmons and Little Jimmy Muldoon were sitting in Kat's Jeep on the back driveway next to the old barn, Kat's head was spinning with all that Jimmy had just told her, and she was having second thoughts about the spontaneous three-hour journey from the safety of her Lake County home. Yes, Kat sorely regretted her rash decision to drive Little Jimmy to the source of many nightmares without first calling her husband, Deputy Ron Simmons. A shiver ran through her at the realization that no one knew they were at the vacant Mare Vista estate. At least, Kat *hoped* it was vacant! *That thought* sent a shudder through her entire petite body.

"It's okay Kat. I'm with you," Jimmy said protectively. "I heard about what happened to you here, but we'll be okay. I promise."

Surprise morphed into suspicion as Kat turned to look squarely at the teenager whom she once hoped to adopt, "How do *you* know about *that* LJ?" Kat asked the boy, using the nickname his foster brothers called him.

LJ responded by lifting one eyebrow and giving her a sly grin as he opened his door. "Come on! Let's go get the documents," he said, as he slid out of the Jeep.

"Well, if we're going to do this, we better get started," Kat conceded, reluctantly giving way to curiosity. She was again surprised when Little Jimmy *led her* over the fence and through the barn to the secret tunnel door. "I've got a map," was all LJ said to her questioning look.

They were midway through the tunnel, when Jimmy paused. Putting his finger on his lips, he

1

motioned Kat to be still. Kat turned off her flashlight. The two stood frozen, listening to the sound of murmuring. They were not alone in the tunnel. Kat saw a flash of light, and heard the familiar rusty creaking coming from the ladder that led up to the trap door into the basement ahead, which caused a terrifying flashback. Jimmy reached for her hand.

Fighting back panic, and grabbing hold of Jimmy's hand, Kat started to pull him back towards the barn, but a second flashlight coming quickly towards them from that direction cut her short. A scream escaped Kat's tightly clenched teeth, as terror filled her very being.

"I'm sorry Kat," she heard Jimmy say quietly, "I *had* to go along with this."

Stunned into a daze, Kat followed the young man she had always held so dearly to her heart. "This is the only way," LJ said and tossing his lit flashlight far into a drainage tunnel, he pulled Kat to the floor and firmly shoved her through the opening. It was so small she could barely crawl through on her stomach. After about three feet, the drainage tunnel gradually widened so she was able to rise to hands and knees and crawl. All the while Jimmy was pushing her and urging her to hurry. Finally, the tunnel opened up wide enough to stand. Jimmy picked up his flashlight, sprang to his feet, grabbed Kat's hand and pulled her to her feet, all in what seemed to her was in one motion. He tugged the stunned woman along through the tunnel until he suddenly shoved her against the wall of a shallow alcove, and covered her whimpering mouth with his hand. "Shh! Don't move a muscle!" LJ ordered sternly.

The only thing Kat could do was obey. As she complied, her only thought was, "When did Little Jimmy's hand get so big?" Her last thought as everything went black was, "I didn't ask Little Jimmy the right questions…"

PART 1

CHAPTER ONE

BEGINNING OF THE END

Lake County Deputy Sheriff Lenard and his underling and niece's husband, Deputy Ron Simmons, had been called to a stake out by Private Eye Jack Moran, who had been working with them on an ongoing case. A tip, which came from an anonymous caller, said the items they needed had been split up so if one was found it was no good without the other; he said it was imperative to get to the two locations immediately because several people were bidding on them. The information led Lenny to an area on Cobb Mountain in the green belt where the three of them had spent months searching for hidden documents, journals, and perhaps a buried treasure of some sort. Ron and Jack were led to another remote mountainous region, where they split up to get to cover as much ground as quickly as possible. Jack came upon an old wooden box hidden in plain sight, and called out to Ron. The box contained old, yellowed, but useless documents. Looking through the contents, Ron shook his head and grumbled.

Jack echoed Ron's grumbling, "I know. This was too easy."

"Yeah," Ron replied, "Someone planted this to draw us here, but why?" He was still speaking as his cell phone rang.

Ron answered and listening for a moment he paled, hung up and took off in a dead run up the trail through the woods toward Jack's new Jeep Rubicon. Without a word, Jack followed while using the remote start.

Ron didn't speak for a few moments while Jack maneuvered his Rubicon out of the thicket where he'd hidden it. Then as Jack drove, Ron tried calling his wife's Uncle Lenny, but just got a busy circuit signal.

Several weeks later...

Over a month had passed since Kat's disappearance. The last call into Kat's cell phone was from LJ's cell phone. And the last ping on her phone was from a tower above Silverado Trail near the small Napa Valley town of St. Helena, about an hour and half after Jimmy's call.

Ron had called the Lombardis, who said although LJ had not returned from hiking, it was not unusual behavior for him. He often got caught up in his research on Mount Hannah. Lombardi said if he didn't show up, they'd let Ron know, but they were sure he was fine.

Guido had laughed, "You know how obsessed he gets. He's probably camping out while buried in research for his ecology project," as he hung up the phone. Ron didn't like his choice of words.

INLAWS AND OUTLAWS

Kat's mom and sister, Caroline, and Angel Amoretti, had offered early on to help Ron with the baby. Ron at first declined their offer, but finally had to relent when he returned to work. Kat's Uncle Lenny and

Auntie Antoinette were constantly popping in for moral support as well.

Ron was once again grateful to have married into a tight knit family, though for the time being he seemed to be withdrawn—keeping them at arm's length. Especially Lenny's wife, whom he once adored. More than once she left teary-eyed when Ron rejected her attempts to watch the baby, whom he had become fiercely protective of.

Ron finally accepted his mother-in-law's and sister-in-law's offer to move into the downstairs guest quarters, and had taken over most of the care of Baby Ronnie, even when Ron was home.

The family settled into a routine. Ron of course was home every moment possible, hovering over his son, while Caroline and Angel attended to the housekeeping. Lenny was there for Ron to unload on, while Auntie kept the entire family fed. Ron's stepdad, Bill Norris, who was chief investigator for the Attorney General's Office of the State of California, visited when he was able to leave Sacramento and called every evening.

Although surrounded by family helped, Ron was obviously worried and understandably edgy. He tried to stay calm and go about his business, as he followed the investigation as closely as he could. Early on, High Sheriff Buchanan, taking his usual authoritative hands-on-hips stance, had told him and Lenny in no uncertain terms that they were too close to the investigation to be involved. He promised to give them daily updates, leaving no room for debate.

Buchanan had never been supportive of what he called, "Ron's extracurricular investigations." But this was personal for Ron. And he felt Buchanan's disinterested and detached attitude toward the disappearance of a fellow lawman's—let alone his subordinate's—wife, unprofessional to say the least.

The strain of the job was taking its toll on Ron, and it had expanded to his home life as well. It wasn't helpful that Angel's beau, John Buchanan, the sheriff's son, was a frequent visitor.

It bothered Ron to have the high sheriff's kid underfoot. He needed space. But it appeared the younger Buchanan wanted to take the relationship with Ron's sister-in-law to the next level. He was pushing the courtship ahead more quickly than Angel wanted at the moment. This also bothered Ron. For one thing, Ron was reminded of his own exciting courtship with Kat, which hurt to think about right now. Secondly, he felt that John was being inconsiderate of Angel at this time of family crisis.

Ron had overheard Angel say to her mother, "You'd think he would be more empathetic to my feelings and stop pushing for... At first, I thought he had walked in from the deck, and she stopped short. But Ron heard enough to know she had tired of the 'self-absorbed *pretty boy*,' which is what Kat had called him shortly after her sister started dating him.

Not dating, really. John just started showing up to hang out while Angel worked with the boys and horses at the Lombardi's foster home.

Angel, who had always loved horses, had been learning about using horses as therapy for children, and had decided to go in that direction professionally after graduating from college. It had become her obsession. Angel, it seemed, had become John Buchanan's.

Since LJ was the only boy left in the Lombardi's foster home, and he was camping, there was no need for Angel to go to the Lombardi's. So now it seemed John had moved his courtship to Ron's home. As much as Angel tried to discourage John, he was relentless. Ron decided to keep John engaged in conversation, letting his young sister-in-law withdraw to her room to wait for John to leave. John seemed oblivious, and appeared to enjoy Ron's conversation, almost as though he'd come to see *him*. Ron had no patience with John trying to 'talk shop' with him. "He may be the son of a sheriff, but he has no concept of what the job entails," Ron growled as he watched John's pickup crawl up the driveway one evening after he finally left.

"Maybe John thinks it's a male bonding thing, and he's trying to get close to Angel's family," Caroline suggested, causing Angel to stick her finger into her open mouth and exaggerate gagging.

"Maybe," was all Ron said, and walked out on the deck to look at Mount Konocti. Ron frowned at the mountain, and growled quietly, "Looks to me like John has been sent by his father to keep tabs on me. The punk has even tried to 'question' me as to how Kat and I have been getting along." Then looking at his watch, Ron reached in his pocket for his cell phone and called his dad.

Time passed slowly for Ron. It had now been two months since Kat vanished, and yet there had not been any press releases; no announcements by the Sheriff's Department whatsoever. And no word from the Lombardis about Jimmy. And although Ron met with Sheriff Buchanan daily, he had not been able, or maybe he was just unwilling, to provide Ron with any updates about his wife.

It was hard on Ron to sit back and see things around him returning to normal. It was difficult, too, for him to watch business as usual return for the various individuals and entities whom he long suspected were, if not directly involved with, delighted by his wife's disappearance.

Ron tried to obey the orders of the high sheriff, and keep himself busy with his duties as a deputy sheriff, and leave the investigation to the detectives assigned to the case. But from what he could discern, they were writing it off as a domestic dispute, or an overwhelmed young mother who needed to take time off from her own job and family life due to stress. More and more, Ron heard, "Just relax. She'll probably turn up shortly, having just gone somewhere for some R and R." Ron overheard a couple of fellow deputies talking in the lunchroom as he walked in, "Didn't she do that before?" "Yeah," the other deputy laughed, "She pulled a disappearing act when Ron tried to set the wedding date?"

Although those words stung Ron severely, and more than angered him, he tried with all his might to stay calm and ignore the gossip and innuendos. That is until one day, the words took a new direction.

Women's clothing and other items had been discovered by a hiker in a ravine off Harrington Flat Road on Cobb Mountain, as if tossed from a vehicle. Ron had been called in to identify the items. He recognized the sweater, brush, and makeup bag to be things Kat had kept in her office at work. "There would have been no reason she would have stopped at her office the day of her disappearance," he'd told Buchanan.

"Unless she didn't want to go home for some personal items," was the high sheriff's gruff response. "We have a witness who said Kat was in quite a state when she showed up late for her *support group* at Crossroads Inn the day you said she went missing."

Instead of opening up an investigation of a high-risk missing person, the high sheriff more or less put a gag order on the entire situation. Just when Ron thought it couldn't get worse, it did! Because it now seemed Ron was "a person of interest," in his wife's disappearance.

"How could anyone suspect Ron of harming the person he loves most in the world?" Angel demanded loudly upon hearing the latest rumors from John Buchanan. "No one who knows Kat and Ron should even give these ugly rumors a second thought, let alone *repeat them*!" she shouted as she stormed out of the room.

After several moments of silent glares from Caroline, John for the first time seemed to understand that his presence wasn't appreciated as much as he had thought. Stammering, he offered a lame excuse about something he needed to do and left.

"How dare he!" demanded an angry Caroline, as John's pickup disappeared up the driveway for the last time. Caroline turned to offer a consoling hug to her son-in-law.

CHAPTER TWO

TWO PARTIES AT CROSSROADS

PRELUDE TO A PARTY

Deputy Ron Simmons stared intently at the local newspaper writeup in the upcoming events column that was announcing an exclusive gala event to be held at Crossroads Inn Time B&B and Spa. "The last place Kat had been seen," Ron thought ironically.

The writer had speculated on who would be attending the *by invitation only* event, listing Jim Bradford Drye, the CEO, and the unnamed Board of Directors of The Fumaroles on Cobb Mountain and their plus-ones. Others on the guest list were several locals including the High Sheriff Buchanan and his son John; Eugene Smith, a new Lake County attorney and his plus-one, Linda Amoretti; Guido and Francesca Lombardi; Dr. Richard Fleming and his plus-one; William Melbourne and Wendy Jones Melbourne; and some out-of-the-county people: Lorenzo and Angie Annunzio; Vince and Stella Lombardi; John and Lois Amoretti; and Ralph Henderson and his plus-one, as possible guests.

Also included in the writeup was a mouthwatering five-course exotic menu. "Other than that, not much is known, except that this will probably be the most elaborate event Lake County has seen in decades!" the writer concluded.

"Except, also for the fact that most of the guest list were headliners for dubious reasons not so long ago in this very newspaper." Ron muttered and scowled.

Officer Simmons often stopped by on his rounds to chat with the prominent owners of the elegant Crossroads Inn Time B&B and Spa. And they, like most business owners, appreciated being checked in on. But Ron and his wife, Kat Simmons, had a special relationship with Catarina and Eduardo Spidiacci. Not only had they been especially helpful in the past with investigations Ron had been involved in, but Kat had joined a self-help group that met regularly at the Inn.

But this was no routine visit, though Ron tried to appear nonchalant when he stopped by Crossroads on his rounds around the lake to chat with Eduardo Spidiacci. After brief greetings, Ron mentioned the newspaper announcement. Eduardo confirmed that yes, the plans for an elaborate and gala party were being painstakingly planned, and that Catarina was determined to carry out every detail impeccably. The innkeeper did not seem surprised to have already received back most of the RSVPs, all checked attending.

"Well, it certainly seems to be causing a lot of buzz," Ron replied with cold eyes.

"Yes, I think it'll prove to be the most successful event Crossroads has ever seen. And I know the most elaborate!" Eduardo said as he proudly showed off one of the beautifully engraved gold invitations, which had been sent out to an elite and private guest list.

Ron read the invitation silently:

**YOU AND A PLUS-ONE ARE
CORDIALLY INVITED TO JOIN A
SELECT FEW
INVESTORS TO A GALA EVENING OF
CHAMPAGNE, MUSIC, AND GOURMET
FOOD, AT THE EXCLUSIVE
CROSSROADS INN TIME
TO REVEAL A MUCH-ANTICIPATED
SPECIAL PROJECT INVOLVING
THE FUTURE OF
THE FUMAROLES ON
COBB MOUNTAIN**

TICKETS-- $2500. per person

**RSVP with check to:
CROSSROADS INN TIME B&B and SPA**

Ron stared at the words then locked eyes with Eduardo's. Though Eduardo's lips were smiling, his eyes were ice-cold as he stared back into Ron's squinting eyes.

A low whistle came from Ron's lips but his eyes remained cold. "Five thousand a couple."

"Yep Ron, and we received checks with each RSVP." Eduardo quipped trying not to sound glib, "everyone's expecting quite the reveal party."

"How's the plans coming along for your gala event?" Ron asked trying to sound nonchalant, but it came out sarcastic. "The plans coming along okay?" he added.

"Yeah. Everything's going as planned, so far so good. Like I said, got most of the RSVPs back. Not surprising, Sheriff Buchanan was first to accept. No doubt he is expecting this party to provide the perfect networking opportunity for campaign schmoozing he is so fond of. Maybe even the platform for an announcement of his own. I heard he is already front runner as candidate for the congressional seat." Ron just nodded, and began walking toward his patrol car and as his usual custom, the innkeeper accompanied him to his car, lingering in his goodbyes.

It was getting harder and harder to abstain from commenting on the political climate infecting Lake County. But Ron had other things—more important things—on his mind. He wouldn't allow himself to get distracted with the upcoming election, no matter *how much* he disliked the candidate. After a bit more short-talk, Ron paused to look up at the clouds gathering in the sky.

"What about the other event?" Ron's voice cracked as he asked. Eduardo just nodded, and Ron took his leave.

TIME TO LAUGH and TIME TO MOURN

Finally, the big night arrived and, as customary for Catarina, the final touches on the tables for the outdoor gala event were done personally. But her usual enthusiasm was missing. Her flower arrangements were missing her signature touch of a daisy or two, as well. Instead, each table held one eighteen-inch black orchid, accompanied by a deep red rose. Her usual swan napkins were also replaced by black napkins folded into fans. It was obvious she didn't much like the people who would be recipients of her outdoor hospitality that evening.

Simultaneously, the inn had an indoor event that was just as unpleasant for Catarina to host. But for a much different reason.

14

The mood in the huge library was somber. Catarina greeted her guests at the library door and pointing to a nearby table asked them to turn off their cell phones and label them with the pre-printed ID stickers before depositing them into a large basket.

Although there had yet to be an announcement of Kat Simmons' disappearance, her closest family and friends were gathered together to remember her in the dimly-lit library of Crossroads Inn. Images of Kat in happier days flashed on the huge screen that had been pulled from the ceiling, as her friends tried not to look through the large bay windows at the parade of headlights slowly creeping up the driveway. The irony of watching Kat's enemies arrive for a celebration of greed and corruption didn't escape Angel's notice.

"A celebration of sadness and gladness on the same night. At the same venue. How ironic. How painfully, excruciatingly ironic." Angel said, and turned her head from the window, lifting a hankie to her wet and swollen eyes. Ron patted her hand, but he also had a difficult time swallowing as he thought of the gloating fat cats in the arriving limos. As the patio below filled with the elegant partygoers, their laughter could be heard inside by the small group of mourners. Mrs. Capra, whose tears were slowly turning into rage, finally voiced what the others were feeling: "Can someone please tell me *WHO* scheduled our gathering at the same time as..." her voice trailed off as she locked eyes with Catarina's.

THE GALA REVEAL PARTY

Limos lined the long driveway all the way past the gates of Crossroads Inn Time B&B and Spa

15

while waiting their turn to deliver their elite passengers.

The limo doors were opened and tuxedo clad men stepped out and assisted glamorously attired and bejeweled women. Both were welcomed and led through the main entrance of the inn, out onto the veranda to the top of the stairs where a butler stood tall. Next to the butler were a couple of attendants who were collecting and labeling cell phones and checking coats, before the butler called out the names of couples as they filed down the stairs to the lower terrace where the festivities would soon start.

At the bottom of the stairs, a maître d' formally greeted each couple as a waiter stepped forward to lead them to their table, where they found a token attached to their place card. The guests mused over the tokens, laughing and joking as they shared with each other the whimsical tokens.

The night was magical, filled with excitement and anticipation of a life-changing event that would be announced after dinner, as the invitation had promised. Low-lit pink twinkle lights covered trees and pillars, filling the night air with a pink glow. A gourmet five-course dinner had been planned and was being prepared to perfection in the kitchen. As wine was poured, the first course was served, which were mouth-watering hors d'oeuvres of mango, apple, and mint salsa served on a gourmet cracker selection and topped with melted brie. An orchestra played softly while a singer crooned from the veranda. As forks were placed on empty plates, a waitperson appeared to remove them from view.

As the last plate was removed, suddenly the music stopped, lights dimmed, and a drum roll announced the second course. A spotlight danced around the veranda as shadowy figures moved into formation. The spotlight stopped on the waitpersons who were posed in rows on three stairs to form a pyramid. The musical crescendo rose and colored floodlights lit the water fountains as they swayed and danced to the beat. The mouth-watering second course of the promised five-course gourmet meal was dramatically served to each guest, consisting of curried beef-vegetable samosas and portobello goat cheese phyllo pouches, served with a traditional raita yogurt dip.

No sooner were the plates removed when once again the lights dimmed and shadowy figures were seen forming a pyramid at the top of the stairs. When the lights went up, the third course of Asian julienne salad with cilantro and cracked peanuts, served with a marinated, pan-seared, then broiled pork tenderloin brochette were served by the skilled and graceful waitpersons. The 'ahhhs' grew louder with each course.

The main course of apricot, almond, and wild-rice-stuffed half Cornish hen, served with a carrot and leek mashed Yukon potato, asparagus with roasted balsamic pearl onions, and sweet bell peppers, were served in the same delightful manner.

A short intermission between the main course and dessert was filled with the singer crooning loudly. While some of the diners freshened up in the nearby gentlemen's room and ladies' powder room, several other couples took to the dance floor.

The music stopped and the singer left the stage, signaling the guests to return to their tables.

The lights again dimmed and a bright, lively light and water show lit up the patio as waitpersons delivered the final course: Jack Daniels chocolate chip pecan pie, served with Chantilly cream.

As dessert plates were cleared, the lights dimmed even more and the orchestra suddenly went quiet.

LIGHTS CAMERAS ACTION!

Inside the library, the teary-eyed mourners who had been trying to focus on the video of Kat's life were stunned when the screen suddenly changed to a closed-circuit TV. Kat's friends and family found themselves watching the elite assembly of Lake County's Who's Who finishing dinner.

The outside lights went low as a drum roll came from the orchestra. Catarina had been with the mourners in the library all evening, but now they were surprised when her voice was suddenly heard coming soft and sweet as honey through speakers strategically hidden in the branches, inviting the glamourous guests below to go to the amphitheater. "Traitor!" Lenny muttered in the library.

As the colored floodlights from the water fountains came back up, ushers in white jackets led the giddy guests, each clutching their token, up a lit path to the bleachers. Hidden cameras following their every step. The elegant guests were seated on plush cushions dressing the long-curved cement benches, overlooking the darkened stage below.

Though still unseen, Catarina's gentle calm voice was again heard, now from the trees surrounding the bleachers, welcoming them all to the amphitheater:

"Tonight, it will be on this very stage, where so many concerts, dance recitals, and plays have been acted out for many decades, that the climax of the evening will play out, in the form of a board game—and you are the players!" Catarina's voice called out, sweetly. As the lights were brought up, barely audible exclamations were uttered by delighted guests upon seeing the stage painted like a colorful board game. Not all the guests were called to the game. Only the ones holding specific tokens were invited to bring their token and to take their corresponding place on the board, one square representative of each token.

THE GAME

Though still unseen, it seemed clear to all that Catarina would be the Master of Ceremonies of the game.

Her voice, now not so soft, laughed: "There's not too many after dinner activities more enjoyable than a good board game. *Welcome to The Game!*" The guests giggled at the mysterious game they were all to be a part of and anxiously awaited instructions.

"As you've no doubt noticed the stage is an elaborate gameboard. You all are on specific squares marked by the token you hold. As with all games, there are rules. The rules to this game are: when The Master of The Game calls out a token, the holder is asked a question and has 60 seconds to answer it. For each incorrect *or unanswered* question, the player must move to the next square. The final move is into a large square painted white with black stripes or 'bars' big enough for all—called JAIL, and the winner… well, the winner *gets it all!*"

This brought a chuckle from all the players, as though it was an inside joke.

Catarina continued loudly as she announced: "Tonight's game is called, 'Ask the Right Questions, To Get the Right Answers.'"

The participating guests smiled widely at their dates, who clapped from the bleachers, thinking they already had all the answers.

They all, players and audience alike, waited with bated breath for Catarina to ask the first question.

Colored spotlights flashed and danced around the stage, while a low drum roll could be heard coming from the orchestra back on the terrace.

Then silence. Thick, dark silence.

Finally, Catarina's sweet voice filled the dark amphitheater to reveal the question.

"The question tonight of course is: 'What is your connection to…'" Catarina paused, as flood lights lit the amphitheater shining on the smiles spreading across the faces of the players, clearly expecting her to say "The Fumaroles on Cobb Mountain."

However, Catarina's voice had now changed from the light and playful tone to a more serious one, "…Jimmy Muldoon?

A gasp was issued simultaneously from the guests, both from the game players standing on the stage, as well as the guests seated on the bleachers, followed by another thick silence.

A male voice is suddenly heard laying out the ground rules for the game, causing a sudden outpouring of shocked murmurings that drowned out the young man's words.

"The thing is," the young voice continued, creating another round of loud murmurings among the guests, both those in the amphitheater as well as those in the library. "Yes, the thing is," the voice repeated when the murmuring ceased, "since you all are somehow here because of... well *Jimmy Muldoon*, and the answers to most of the mysteries seem to lead to *Jimmy Muldoon*... the first question must be: 'What's your interest in Jimmy Muldoon? Just how are you connected to... or perhaps *related* to...?'" the voice paused, as another hush spread through the guests. After a moment or two, he continued, "Jimmy Muldoon. While you are considering that question, I'll be calling out specific questions to help you focus on your answer—to ones holding specific tokens." It seems the tokens weren't as random as the shocked guests had first thought.

The youthful voice continued, "The first question will be directed to a couple who are each holding a boy token. This couple made the Lake County scene several years ago, gathering adoring fans as a result of all their contributions to the county—especially to the weak and helpless youth of Lake County. To the couple holding the boy tokens...", as the question was being announced a particular couple seem to recognize the voice. The stunned couple froze, mouths agape. "... the question is in regards to the husband, first of all, concerning a very large estate—which has been left untouched, and intact, with you in sole control... that is, ever since it was your testimony that led the two previous heir-intendeds to be put in jail... Incidentally those two people are now out of jail on early parole— thanks to the help of a well-known local official. But what surprised me is that they seemed to have also been welcomed back with opened arms by none other than *you*! So, my question for you is: Who exactly is the rat in the family? Is it one or both of those siblings who were once heir-apparent… or perhaps your young wife? Or is it you? Or just maybe… it's not any *one* of you, but *all of you*! Which is it?"

Catarina's voice interrupted, "Times up! Move to next square, please." The man seemed eager to comply, hoping the limelight would be off him, but The Master of The Game was not yet finished with him.

"Perhaps, the four of you were reunited because there is something *or someone* who has come to your attention that threatens to expose the fact that the estate in question was never legally obtained by your family. When exactly did you learn that the estate was taken illegally by a mob-run real estate legal firm, and that there exists a living heir who can, at any moment, snatch it from your greedy hands? Yes, who told you there was a person with the right credentials and *bloodline* to affect your control of, not just the estate, but every dime ever made off it? Was it your wife?" The usual suave and debonair man holding the boy token was at a loss for words. "And exactly what is the name of the legal heir whose existence threatens to oust you?" Looking at his wife, he remained awkwardly silent.

A loud squawking emitted from the speakers, followed by Catarina's voice, "Aww. Times up! But thank you for playing, sir. You may move directly to *jail!*"

The man's wife smiled demurely, when The Master of The Game said, "I'll save your question for later." Unlike her husband, she had regained her composure rather quickly, and looked quite innocent; but as she turned away, Ron caught an ever-so-brief smug expression cross her pretty face, as she exchanged quick glances with a guest who was standing a few feet away on the board.

Two contestants on adjoining squares, each holding tokens in the shape of a slice of pie, were the next to be questioned. "It seems appropriate to question you together, since you were both victimized as children by the same woman who betrayed your mother, seduced your father, and stole his affection that he once had bestowed on you both. Yes, sadly you spent your life trying to win back that love, and when he died, you did your best to uncover the diabolical plot wielded against your family by another family. The family whose matriarch formed a vendetta that each generation since has sworn to carry out. The vendetta didn't end when you were both convicted of crimes you never committed and sent to prison. No—the vendetta must be carried on until the last of your bloodline is ended. But one must wonder exactly who started the ball rolling to slide open the prison gates… yes, that is my question to you: How, why, and by whom were strings pulled to win your early and rather abrupt parole from prison? What could have enticed you to join forces with those who set you up?

"Let's examine the facts… well, that is to say we could *RE*-examine the facts. They are public knowledge and easy to find—if you know where to look. And obviously *someone* knows. You joined

23

forces with your enemy in order to save the pie… even though you were only going to get a small piece, it was more than nothing. And it was better than serving your full prison sentence. After all was said and done, you'd have another shot at getting more of the pie. All was going according to plan… *But then enter Kat Simmons*. She was an unwelcomed participant by all sides of the game. All the participants here tonight took their opportunity to try and eliminate her from their game. Chasing her off the mountain until she lost control and rolled her little sports car, trying to run over her in Lakeport, and chasing her through and away from one estate after another, isn't that right? And yet it was the two of you… a brother and sister team who took the fall. Or were you shoved?" the voice of the obvious Master of The Game finally relented much to the obvious relief of the siblings who were standing side by side on the board game. Their relief was only momentary.

"Even though you hated the other participants," the voice began again with renewed firmness, "*and vice versa* there was something that you needed to happen. *You all* needed it to happen so badly that you were able to cast aside the past to ensure the future. And that something was for a certain someone to disappear. Well, actually *two someones*, now since—well—you know. *Kat Simmons*. What a relentless force to deal with, wasn't she? Kat's brilliance and tenacity to solve mysteries… well, she just had to go, didn't she?

"But Kat wasn't who you wanted dead the most… in fact the person you *needed* dead... the one *particular* person who stands between you and millions of dollars is… Who is that one person?" the Master of The Game demanded to know.

The two co-contestants stared defiantly at the loudspeaker that hung low from a tree as The Master of The Game spoke, but visibly jumped at the squawking noise followed by Catarina's voice "Oooh, sorry time's up. But do play again!"

Silence and confusion seemed to spread through the library, where most of the guests knew of the harrowing experiences suffered by Kat over the past several years. She had been chased off Cobb Mountain several times; and followed clues that led her to experience horrifying terror in the basement and tunnel of Mare Vista.

Kat's mother, Caroline Amoretti was confused. "But if it was more than just those two… *who else* was chasing Kat?" she stammered.

"How did that one person cross your radar," The Master of The Game's voice started up again, this time addressing the contestant whose token was a gun, "What should I call you? You've introduced yourself by many names, even here in this small community. How many aliases do you have? How many of those aliases are a hit-man for the mob—or anyone else with the right price? Who was it who first approached you… hired you to try to infiltrate Deputy Ron Simmons' family—to hide your true connections by pretending to be a direct descendant of Captain Samuel Spears? Was it a close associate of a former mob attorney? Or perhaps the mob's current attorney—*or consigliere*? Did your boss, sic you on your new target, as per his usual reasons—to eliminate heirs to properties of interest to the *'Family'*? Or perhaps it was someone else? Someone nearer to home. Someone with a much higher goal. *A much higher goal indeed.* Or, just might it be someone else altogether? Someone dear to all present tonight. Someone who *recruited* you... who *coerced* you... into joining a growing team of assassins? And who did *you* coerce into compromising his loyalty to *his family,* and assist you in locating documents rumored to be hidden on a certain property? Wasn't it the son-in-law and sous chef of that property? But tell me please, who was the person who first contacted you and was directing your moves? Was that person not a distant relative of yours? And in fact, was that person not the puppeteer of the whole plot to bring down families and fortunes? And was there a special reason you were chosen? If you were not able to obtain the much sought-after documents, who did that person order you to erase from the picture? What is the name of that person… or rather *target*?

This was one guest, who seemed not to mind the questions—even relished them. "Well, I can see you've done your homework," the hitman sneered. "But ya betta watch your back. Your tutor just might not be who you think he is," letting out such an evil cackle that even the squawking from the loudspeakers was a welcome sound, as Catarina interjected, "Sorry. Wrong answer!"

Unabashed, The Master of The Game continued, "Perhaps it is *you*, sir, who has been misled by your umm, *informant*. Would it interest you to know that the sous chef in question had a change of heart, and instead took information he gathered from you directly back to Officer Ron Simmons? Would it also interest you to learn that *your* informant found the documents you were so desperate to get your hands on and handed said documents over to Officer Simmons?" At that the evil grin seemed to freeze on the hitman's face like a grotesque mask. "Well," the Master of The Game continued, "I can clearly see you are not ready to answer more questions. Not quite yet, anyway. Perhaps you'll be more cooperative before the evening is over. I think you might be very interested in hearing the response of a certain upcoming contestant."

Catarina interjected a quick and light-hearted, "Moving on, then."

"Salvatore Delilio," this was the first contestant to be named by The Master of The Game "What items did you uncover in the wall of Crossroads Inn B&B? In the wall behind the hand-stitched sampler, besides *Carolina Jane's* second journal? And why did you hold those items back? Wasn't it because you read the journals, letters, and other documents, and discerned that there are two living heirs to Crossroads Inn Time B&B and Spa? And they supersede the will that put your wife's family in ownership of said property? What are the names of those heirs? Isn't one of those heirs the answer to all the questions asked tonight?" Even though the questions were intended to clear Sal of being a perp, Sal just hung his head in shame. The fact that he had indeed at first joined the side of these evil men was something he was sure would never be forgiven by his wife, nor her family.

The next to be questioned was holding a token representing a notebook. "Who was it that hired you to keep track of a certain child? Was it your brother who once ran a local foster home using the name and fingerprints of your husband, and with the help of your husband forced the children in his care, children under your supervision, into slave labor? Or perhaps it was your husband's idea? Or were *you* the mastermind of this sinister scheme, and they both answered to you?" The Master of the Game paused, giving the woman time to lock her glaring eyes with her husband's and then her brother's. "Or was it a man who is now in control of a multi-million-dollar company that belonged to his brother-in-law, William Logan, who had been murdered along with his wife? And wasn't their pregnant daughter kept against her will? And wasn't she told her baby had been delivered a stillbirth? But… well, I don't have to tell you what really happened to *that baby*." Again, the Master of The Game paused momentarily before finishing with a tone much deeper, "Or were you approached by someone else with the idea that a certain person could somehow be *very profitable* to you? What did it take to convince you that perhaps there were people willing to pay a very high price for updates on the whereabouts of that certain child who was the rightful heir to the land upon which a very lucrative business has been in operation for decades? But, once again, there was that woman, the woman who is now missing, who took it upon herself to protect that target of so many people and to investigate the bloodlines leading from the last known legal landowner and follow his bloodline back to the child… the target. What is that *target's name*?"

Again, the stunned silence that followed the Master of The Game's shocking disclosure was broken by the familiar squawk, that screeched from the loudspeakers. Catarina, who by now didn't try to hide her disdain, offered obvious sarcastic condolences, and scoffed: "Sorry, times up *Miss*. Move to next square. But please, *do play again*."

The Master of The Game's tone took quite an unusually powerful and confident turn when addressing the next contestant. "Mr. … hmmm, seems we have another contestant with aliases. What shall I call you? I may as well just call you Mr. Doe. I'll skip over your dubious past and convictions. Let's just address the fact that you were recently released early on parole for those serious crimes, is that correct? Who was it exactly that pulled strings to get you and your wife tonight, along with several *others*, who were released on parole and who were sentenced to many, *many* years in prison? Could it be… yes indeed! I believe it could be the person holding an honorable position and who recently threw his hat into the ring to run for an even more honorable position… But I'll get to him later.

"My questions for you are first: "Were you after the rumored Captain's treasure? Did you imagine it to be gold? Was it your wife who brought a certain child to your attention? Wasn't the child-labor operation that you schemed up only a secondary plan, a plan to facilitate funding to back your primary plan—that of taking over… well, taking over *it all*? Who was the one person vital for your plans to work? What is that person's name?"

Once again, the questions went unanswered and when told to move to the next square, that too was ignored. But the Master of The Game was undeterred.

"My next question is for Jim Bradford Drye. Or JB Drye, as you're called," who was holding a teapot token. "You are the current CEO of the Board of Directors of The Fumaroles on Cobb Mountain, but prior to that position you held a top-level IT position with the Department of Defense," stated the Master of The Game, "isn't that right?" As JB Drye began to squirm, the voice from the speaker began again matter-of-factly, "Resistance to the operation on Mount Hannah by the State of California has disappeared overnight and perhaps that's why so many are here tonight. You all were expecting to hear that the rumors were true and the plant was about to be given full steam ahead." The Master of The Game added wryly, "pardon the pun," before continuing, "but that is confusing to some because…um," there was an exaggerated pause, "How long has the plant been in existence? And in fact, operating and creating and selling steam energy from The Fumaroles on Cobb Mountain?" After clearing his voice with a fake cough, the Master of The Game continued nonchalantly, "Are you aware of a poker game that took place in which the deed to Mount Hannah was won? What was the name of the person who won the deed to Mount Hannah? Wasn't it Donnell Spears? And who lost the deed to Mr. Spears? Wasn't it a Mr. Logan? As Donnell Spears lay dying from a gunshot to the back, didn't he give all his possessions, including documents, in the presence of and documented by the St. Louis sheriff, to his brother Samuel Spears? And wasn't said deed, and accompanied documents, pertaining to Mount Hannah? And wasn't Mr. Logan hung for the murder of Donnell Spears?" There was a long pause before the Master of The Game continued, "And didn't Mr. Logan's brother hire several—both male and female—private detectives to follow Samuel Spears to regain the deed and other documents? The very Logan who was the founder of your firm. How long has your firm been stalking the Spears family? How many years? Isn't that number one hundred? For one hundred years there has always been one or more persons hired to stalk the offspring of Samuel Spears. And to what extent have you gone to keep track of offspring from both the Spears and Logan family tree? What have you and your Board of Directors been willing to do over the years to move ahead with your fracking plans? Would murder be out of the question? Or perhaps I could even ask, how many murders have you ordered? Or maybe you preferred to use your IT skills to ensure certain military personnel were sent to the front lines." The Master of The Game's voice grew louder, "And who is your current target? What is that name?"

Silence filled the amphitheater. The stakes just got higher.

The next question was directed to the person holding a star-shaped token. Not even assuming the authoritative stance he was known for could mask his nervousness. "You have suddenly emerged as the frontrunner for the State of California Congress, with a relatively new, but evidently powerful, local attorney running your campaign and who has obtained the backing of several high-profile locals, am I right? And isn't it also true that all, or at the very least the majority, of your many supporters, both financially and otherwise, are individuals or businesses with intense interest in The Fumaroles on

31

Cobb Mountain?" Again, the interrogator paused briefly. "Exactly who approached you with this scheme to enter the high-stake game of politics and favors? Was it... " the Master of The Game let the tension reach its crescendo before going over the long list of possibilities, beginning with: "the known head of a mob family, or perhaps not someone in the family at all... but someone very close to the family? Someone who had at one time been a family problem, in fact." Although the mob was referred to by the Master of The Game, this was the first time it hit a nerve... made someone angry. Lorenzo Annunzio definitely seemed riled. He was not the only one.

Cursing which emitted from Sheriff Buchanan's tight lips was silenced by the squawking loudspeakers, and Catarina's pseudo sympathetic consoling, "Ooh, clearly not the correct answer, Sheriff. And besides, sorry, but you are way too late. Move one square, please." The high sheriff didn't budge.

"Sheriff Buchanan, perhaps I should've been asking a different line of questioning," the young interrogator continued, "Isn't it correct that your plan of going into politics via The Fumaroles' financial backing has been assured success by... what was the *identity* of the attorney who was running your campaign prior to Mr. Smith? Was he not none other than *Stephen Pinero*? The very Stephen Pinero who had reportedly been the victim of a mob hit. And had not a hitman named Enzo been suspected of that crime? The very same Enzo whom you recently helped get released from prison on an early parole for various other serious crimes, including attempted murder? Has Enzo taken on another contract? Who is the target? And have you promised to cover over the murder, just as you've covered over Kat Simmons' disappearance, when and if it occurs? And what is the name of Enzo's target, Sheriff?"

The interrogator quickly directed his attention to the man holding the knife token. "I see we have Sherriff Buchanan's attorney and campaign manager in our presence. Eugene Smith, Esquire. I understand you specialize in real estate law, Mr. Smith? My first question to you, sir, is: If someone homesteaded land in the 1800s, how valid is that homestead today?" The man just stood there, emotionless. "Step to next square, if you will," the game master ordered. The attorney obeyed.

"Next question: If someone *legally* obtained a deed—even if, say, it was won in a poker game— in the 1800s, how valid is it today?" The man scowled, but did not speak. "Take another square Mr. Smith," the Master of The Game instructed, before moving on to the next question: "If someone is heir to an estate, but is found to be adopted, and the entailment specifies an heir must have a blood connection to the deceased, what would be the only thing that could ensure the inheritance? Wouldn't it be to marry someone who had the right bloodline, and give birth to or sire a legal heir that you could control until they reach legal age?" The man turned his head in the direction of the loudspeaker where the voice emitted, but again said nothing. He did however obey the orders to take another square moving him closer not only to jail, but next to someone who he clearly didn't want to be near. The next question hit a nerve. "If someone stole

33

documents proving an Irish entailment was broken, and those documents turned up decades later, could the rightful heir regain the inheritance?" This time the man couldn't hide his anger.

"Mr. Smith, I'm sure you are aware by now why you were chosen for the token in your hand—the knife. The knife can have a double meaning... as I'm also certain you are well aware of, *Mr. Smith*. A knife can be a useful tool, especially when used by a skillful surgeon to give a fugitive a new lease on life, a new identity, as it were. The knife, can also be, and *too often* has been, used to stab trustful friends and business associates in the back. This too, I'm sure you are fully aware of. Keeping this thought in mind, I ask you, sir, who invited you to this game? No, not the game conducted on stage here, tonight... *The Game!* Who enticed you to crawl out from under the protective rock where you've been hiding the past few years? Who made you the *one offer* you couldn't refuse? Yes, who asked you to play puppeteer—perhaps even convinced you that you *were the puppeteer* in The Game. *The kingpin*, in a game which would not only end the life that so many here tonight have been hoping to end, but reinstate *your own*? How so? By directing a plan so *diabolical*... so *complicatedly corrupt*, that it would absolve you of your past. Wash your hands clean of sins against powerful men... powerful business associates. Especially one particularly powerful and vengeful man, who long put his confidence in you to look out for his and his *family's* interests."

The face of the man whom everyone on the board, and most in the audience, knew as Attorney Eugene Smith, had by now turned first maroon with rage, then suddenly went white with fear, as Mr. Annunzio turned to face him squarely head on. The man's legs went weak, and he literally fell to his knees before the mob family head. His gaping and trembling lips were moving, but nothing came out but silence and drool—or perhaps it was tears, flowing from his eyes and nose past his lips down onto his tuxedo. One thing was certain. Eugene Smith, aka *Steven Pinero*, the one-time Los Gatos attorney, had gotten plastic surgery on his face and fingerprints and had been hiding in plain sight in Lake County. He had actually been managing a satellite office of the mobbed-up law firm where he once worked and where his paralegal girlfriend, Linda, still worked. Linda, who also until recently, worked as a temp at Crossroads Inn where she had been sent to act as a mole and to befriend Kat Simmons. For all the scheming, planning, manipulating, and more than likely bribing, that got the arrogant lawyer from A to Z, Steven Pinero was now clearly pleading for his life.

Up in the library, it was only now that Theo Pinero understood why she was invited to Kat's celebration of life. She was not a widow after all. Her abusive, lying, cheating husband Steven Pinero was alive and well and had continued his illegal schemes and activities under everyone's noses. But what interested her most was the realization that she was no longer broke. When her husband went on the lam with his secretary, he left with not only the mob's money, but most of hers as well. Now that she knew her husband was alive and his whereabouts, she could lien his bank account for the amount he stole from her mother's Trust.

Suddenly, one of Crossroad's own was taken off-guard when he was asked, "James Dominic Lewis, how was it, or better yet, *when* was it you first became acquainted with the identity of the real owner of Crossroads Inn? Was it before or *after* you cut the pages out of the journal?" James stopped mid-step, with one foot slightly in the air, and oddly half balanced. "*Or*… was it much earlier… long before you led Catarina and Eduardo to the vacant inn? When did you learn the story of the Spears connection to Crossroads Inn?" James suddenly put all his weight on the wrong foot and lost his balance completely, falling into a planter, at the feet of one of the waiters.

While James was scampering to his feet, the loud unnerving squawking emitted from the loudspeakers, followed by Catarina's shaky voice, "Times up! But... thank you for playing."

The Master of The Game abruptly turned his attention to another player on the board, "We'd all like to know just how *you* are out of jail and back in control and taking the lead of the company, and wealth, that belonged to Heather Logan's father, the now deceased William Logan. How did you arrange that *Mr. Henderson*? How hard were those strings to pull? Or, perhaps I should ask, *Who* pulled those strings? What brought you back to Lake County after your release? Again, maybe should I say, *who* brought you here? You had connections already to Lake County, didn't you, Mr. Henderson?

"There was a child put into the Lake County foster system as an infant. That child's identity had been switched with another who had been the unfortunate principal in an illegal adoption. A situation that led to the poor child's sad demise, didn't it? This was all part of an elaborate scheme to bury the identity of another infant who took the adopted child's place in the foster system, wasn't it? You couldn't chance killing that child, because there would always be the chance of a body turning up and DNA ran, isn't that correct? DNA that is on file with the State of California, am I correct? You couldn't chance the body of a child to be traced by DNA and connected to a woman who was found dead off a hiking trail on Cobb Mountain, could you, Mr. Henderson?

"Or should I say *Uncle Ralphie?* Is that what Heather Logan called you when you took control of her inheritance after her parents were killed in *an accident*? Or later, when you held her against her will while trying to force her to consent to an abortion? Actually, Uncle *Monster* is, I believe, how she referred to you in her journal. Oh yes! *I've read Heather's journal.* I know how you terrorized her and how she brilliantly escaped with a new identity and location. And yes, I know that she never believed the lie you told. About how her child had been stillborn… I know how hard she searched for her son. How heartbroken she was when she tracked down the pitiful decoy baby purchased by you and placed deliberately in harm's way with forged documentation. Who came up with the plan to hide Heather's child in plain sight… in the foster system? Who picked the social worker to bribe to keep track of the child?

"How you must've panicked when you learned Heather Logan had surfaced in the same obscure out-of-the-way county as her baby. Yes, it must have been terrifying for you, to learn the child's mother, whom you had been searching for, turned up in Lake County. Did you think she had traced her son here? When your private detective got word of an attorney looking into the illegal adoption, how quickly did you find Heather Logan at the retreat on Cobb Mountain? Is that why you decided to find someone to send into the retreat to befriend her? Was that when you approached the high sheriff about expanding his political career? Was it him *or you* that suggested his son go into the retreat for therapy in order to meet Heather Logan? Was it you pulling the strings?"

The Master of The Game had to pause to gain control of his emotions before continuing, "Sadly, that beautiful young mother's life ended before she learned of her child's true whereabouts…. but you know that don't you? Her last act of defiance to your authority was reported back to you, isn't that right, *Mr. Ralph Henderson*?

"You've led the search for your nephew and the woman who took it upon herself to protect him and investigate the bloodlines—bloodlines that will take all power and wealth away from you and give it to the rightfully legal heir—*Heather Logan's son!*" The Master of the Game didn't try to hide the irony in his voice when he added, "Or, perhaps you only thought you were pulling the strings. Would it surprise you to know that you were not actually the puppeteer pulling the strings… orchestrating all that has transpired?

"One last question, sir: What is the name that Heather's son has been using all sixteen years of his life?"

Catarina's voice, not belying her disgust, followed the familiar squawking from the speaker, "Your time is up, *Uncle Ralphie*!"

The Master of The Game now focused on a person referred to earlier, who had smugly sighed with relief thinking he had dodged yet another bullet.

"Lorenzo Annunzio. Head of the Los Gatos Annunzio Family and Los Gatos real estate law firm. With witnesses disappearing, or changing their stories, your law firm has gone untethered for many decades and has been able to continue *acquiring* large estates. Are the rumors true that Crossroads Inn Time B&B and Spa is in your immediate crossfire? When did you come to learn about the connection of Crossroads Inn and The Fumaroles on Cobb Mountain? Who is the one person who has the potential to stand in your way of taking control of both properties?"

GAME OVER

By now there were waiters stationed at every possible exit, who began opening their white jackets to expose guns and FBI badges.

The guests were desperately looking towards the woods beyond the bleachers for an escape. Someone pulled a switch and bright floodlights from the trees filled the arena, blinding the guests, both those onstage as well as those left in the bleachers, as more agents, who had earlier served the guests with food and drink, appeared with handcuffs ready to serve arrest warrants.

And yet, The Master of The Game was not finished interrogating the contestants. "John Buchanan, isn't it true that you temporarily abandoned your playboy status to pursue a relationship with Angel Amoretti, at the behest of your father? And isn't it accurate to say, the purpose of this was to get inside family information, and your hands on documents concerning Captain Samuel Spears' will? Isn't it also true that there was one person who if were not, shall we say, *eliminated*, your father would lose all his financial backing for his campaign, thereby ruining the chances of winning the election he is seeking? What is the name of that *one person*, who could ruin everything for your father and by extension, you?"

Before John could open his mouth, The Master of The Game had moved back to Francesca Carloni Lombardi, "Why did you go to extremes to make sure Kat read the journals and letters of Contessa Carloni and the Myers'? Is it because you wanted her to find out that Contessa's son was stolen and illegally adopted by Myers, hence disqualifying his offspring to be heirs to Mare Vista? Did Maria Carloni, your aunt, come to America to carry out Contessa's vendetta? What were the four family names that Contessa's vendetta was against? Wasn't it Myers, Logan, Spears, and…," again there was a pause before the last name was revealed, "Lombardi?" What were the circumstances of Anthony Lombardi's first wife's death? How long had your great aunt Maria worked for her when she died? Did not her children witness Maria putting powder in her beverages over the course of her last year of life? And did not her children try to bring it to their father's attention? Was it Maria or Sofia Carloni who came up with the plan to infiltrate the Lombardi family through marriage? How long did Anthony—Vince and Stella's father—live after marrying Maria? When did Maria become aware of Anthony's will changes leaving the larger portion of the estate to Guido? Who decided you should marry Guido upon Maria's death? Maria? Sofia? … or did you take it upon yourself to follow your aunt Maria and complete what she had started? To marry into and end the Lombardi bloodline. When you became last of the Lombardi wives, you had surgery to ensure you'd forever remain childless. Yes, the Lombardi bloodline had come to an end, thereby fulfilling that portion of the vendetta. And by leading everyone to the illegal birth certificate and Myers' adoption papers of Contessa Carloni's son, you got a double. And if your plan to frame Ron would have been successful, you would have heaped shame on the Spears family name the way Donnell Spears shamed your family. But something went awry. In this day and age of DNA and family trees, certain names and family lines surfaced. Especially two names. But let's set one aside. There was one particular name… a person surfaced who could throw a hammer into all your planning. All your sacrifices. Who was the one person who stood in the way of your vendetta being complete? Was it not the person who through his triple bloodline would revive the lineage of Spears', Logan's, and Myers'? Was not that person known until today as Jimmy Muldoon?

"In fact, isn't the answer to everyone's final

41

question **James Logan Myers, aka Jimmy Muldoon?"**

One by one, guests tried to slip away, but they were prevented by the attendants from leaving the stage until the game was played out and all questions asked. Floodlights were suddenly turned on, flooding the stage area, blinding anyone who tried to venture climbing down the stairs leading off the stage. It also made further attempts to leave impossible. The only ones remained seated high in the amphitheater were Catarina and Little Jimmy with an FBI agent on either side.

All attendants and waitpersons were members of the FBI. All exits were covered.

The waiting limos had been commandeered by the Feds.

The last words from Little Jimmy, who had been The Master of The Game, to the contestants as they were led away was a triumphant: "GAME OVER!"

CHAPTER THREE

THE INSIDERS

REVEAL AMONG FRIENDS AND FAMILY

After the elaborate gala party's finale, climaxing with the arrest of almost two dozen scoundrels, the real celebration began up in the library where the inside gathering was held.

The atmosphere in the library was like a lightning rod—sparking high with excitement over hearing Jimmy's voice during 'The Game' and knowing he was alive and well. It turned into quite a celebration for Jimmy and gave hope to Kat's family and friends, as well as the Crossroads' staff, who had been replaced by FBI agents and sent to the upper levels of the large Victorian inn. The staff had crowded around open windows while listening intently and watching from darkened rooms, as The Game played out the reveal of many mysteries they had all been wondering about. As the limos, which had been commandeered by the FBI to carry away the couple dozen or so prisoners drove away, Crossroads' employees rushed down to join the guests in welcoming Jimmy back out of exile! And to congratulate him for the courage and strength he displayed while confronting all those powerful people who had been plotting against him. They were all so proud of him!

After many tearful hugs, the mood took an abrupt turn, "But wait!" Mrs. Capra's voice could be heard above the others, "I want to know just who thought this would be fun for us? After weeks of agonizing worry and grief… to put us all though this… this shocking game? Who planned this?" This time she was glaring at Ron, who had just walked in the room and leaned casually against the wall. He involuntarily shrunk further down the wall. The tiny elderly woman still carried a punch with those piercing eyes, causing Ron to remember a stormy night he'd brought Little Jimmy home from a hike on Konocti and met with those icy cold eyes of hers and that sharp tongue.

As Ron pulled himself back up as tall as he could, all eyes were on him. "Alright. Guilty as charged," he tried to joke. No one laughed. He tried a different strategy. "I would've been up here sooner, but I just sent off the last limo of prisoners," reminding all present of the dangerous people whom Little Jimmy had been hiding from. "Catarina had nothing to do with the library dual parties tonight. It was me. Well Jack, Eduardo and me. We met up here under the ruse of planning… well you know. But in reality, we needed a way to get all the perps in one place and off-guard—and we thought allowing all of you to witness them being 'brought down' was well… I thought you all deserved to see it."

"Humph, I should've known it would be men who thought this up!" growled Mrs. Capra.

Shaken a bit, Ron continued, "I may have been wrong, but there it is nonetheless—it's done. The Game part—*that* was Catarina's brilliant idea. Jimmy, of course comprised the questions." After an anticipating hush replaced the murmuring, Ron continued, "Actually it was Jimmy and his… his friend." Again, Ron paused knowing this would cause an uproar among the guests, all whom had a warm spot in their hearts for the rambunctious lad whom they watched grow into such a fine young man... and for whom they felt a tinge of sympathy due to his being an *orphaned foster child*. But to suddenly hear that he helped put together a situation that would cause them even more pain than they had already been enduring was just too much for them to hold in!

"Wait! Did you say, 'Little Jimmy's friend'?" Mrs. Capra said, "All his foster brothers have moved away. I'm not aware of him making any new friends. And he visited me just before he disappea…"

After realizing his mistake in mentioning a newcomer had helped in the investigation, Ron quickly interrupted, "Jimmy will share the details, when and if he wishes, but he's given me permission to share with his closest friends and loved ones the following information...which is to be kept confidential until Jimmy says otherwise." The last part was stated in such a way that everyone present felt obliged to nod in agreement and brought silence to the room.

Ron continued, "Bill Norris had filed a sealed injunction to place Jimmy in special custody while the investigation proceeded. He had arranged for Jimmy to finish the school year online, with a teacher from the California State Board of Education presiding over his finals. Which he, of course aced," he said proudly. "So another fear of Jimmy's was squelched—that of not finishing school because he not only finished the school year, but earned an early diploma!" Ron gave Jimmy a nod.

HOW I SPENT MY SUMMER VACATION

Jimmy reluctantly stood up to face the crowded library. The brave young man of less than an hour ago, suddenly appeared shy and worried that everyone would stay mad at him. "I'm sorry. I didn't mean to scare anyone. There just wasn't any other way," he apologized.

"It's really great LJ that you finished high school. That's wonderful! You've faced so many challenges in your young life as an orph…" Caroline stopped mid syllable. "So you're a high school graduate! How wonderful! And to graduate early, well, that's quite an accomplishment!" Caroline knew the chances of a foster child getting a high school diploma were low.

Caroline's praises caused the boy to straighten up and proudly announce, "And yes, I have a diploma!" Jimmy took a sip of punch and knowing Mrs. Capra could tell he and Ron were holding back a secret, he began to tell his friends gathered there in the library about how he met a new friend.

"One day, I was exploring the mountains and hills below Mount Hannah, and I saw someone watching me. It scared me at first, but he just sat there waiting for me to make the first move. He looked familiar. I finally asked who he was, and he just said: 'Oh, you must've seen me around. I've been to the children's museum several times. I'm very interested in geology and ecology, too.' And we talked quite a while about the mountains and lakes in Lake County. Then another time he said, 'Since you were a little guy, I've been keeping an eye on you. I'm proud of the young man you've become. Your mother would be proud of you.' It stunned me, but also made me

46

curious. I asked him how he knew about her. He said he was her friend. Close friend. He said she was a beautiful and brilliant person and they met while hiking on Mount Hamilton above San Jose. He said, 'That's where she lived. San Jose. We used to walk together around the mountains around San Jose. Mount Hamilton, Loma Prieta, and Mount Umunhum.' Then he said my mother loved rocks. She collected rocks. Especially volcanic rocks. Like me!" Jimmy beamed. "She had once wanted to be a geologist, like I used to, but she became obsessed with ecology—like I am." Jimmy took a breath before continuing proudly, "He said he'd seen me give my dissertations at the Children's Museum. 'Impressive.' He said '*Impressive*!' And he said he was my Watcher." Jimmy leaned back on the table and grinned at everyone. "I know, it sorta worried me, too. I mean who wants someone stalking you like that? Right?" he chuckled. "But it wasn't like that. It wasn't weird at all. It was more like he was watching over me." The more LJ talked about him, the more he was compelled to keep talking. It was like he was hearing it *himself* for the first time. "Sometimes when I was growing up and felt alone, I'd get this strong feeling that there was someone who cared about me… I mean, even before I met Mrs. Capra, Ron, and Kat. Anyway, I kept running into him on the mountain, and each time he told me a little more about himself. How he had been engaged, but had to go to the Gulf War, and he was captured right away, and was a POW for quite a while. Things happened to him that sorta messed up his mind for a while. And when he finally got back home, he looked for his fiancée but he found out she had died. And that she had had a baby boy. *His baby*. Things in her life had been rough and he wished he hadn't had to leave her. He wished he could have been there for her. To help her. He said he looked for his son and it took a long time, but he finally found him." Jimmy wiped a tear from his cheek with the back of his hand. The room was silent. He searched the faces of the people in the library as if he didn't know if he should keep talking.

Finally, LJ's eyes met with Ron's and he felt calmer. And strong again. The young teenager took another deep breath and said, "He didn't tell me at first. He waited until I felt comfortable around him. He finally told me why he'd been keeping an eye on me. He said he knew things were bad for me growing up, but he did what he could do without being caught. He said there was a reason he had to stay behind the scenes. But then he found out there were bad people planning to hurt me. And by that time, I knew it, too. So, he came up with a plan and when the time was right, we would talk to Ron about helping us with our plan. In the meantime, we hiked and camped together and he told me things I sorta already knew, about the people around me. Like Guido and Francesca. I knew when my foster brothers started being sent away, something was going to happen to me. *Something bad*. That's why I started spending more and more time on the mountain with him. And sometimes we'd go to places he'd gone with his fiancée. And we'd stay in a big vacant house he knew about. Mare Vista.

"But one day he told me… it wasn't just me that was in danger. He said something bad was going to happen to Kat if we didn't do something fast. He told me he needed to talk to her. So, he started following her…"

Jimmy became emotional so Ron stepped in, "Jimmy's dad was one of the people who followed and chased Kat on Cobb Mountain." Realizing he let the cat out of the bag, Ron stammered, "He didn't mean to scare her, he was just trying to get her alone, somewhere safe, to talk to her. He knew her phones were tapped, and there were people around her—and me—who were not to be trusted."

The library was quiet for a few moments. What followed was a true lightning bolt of emotions and reactions.

First was Mrs. Capra exclaiming, "Did you say Jimmy's dad?" standing to her feet, then quickly reaching one hand behind her searching for the arm of the chair to ease herself back down on it.

ORPHAN NO MORE

"Mama Capra!" Little Jimmy cried, worried the news was too much for her in her fragile condition, and fearing another stroke. Little Jimmy rushed to her side and tried to calm his former foster mother, "Mama Capra. It's ok. It's okay," he said kneeling to hug her. "You don't have to worry about me anymore, I have a father. But you will always be my Mama Capra! Please be happy for me. He's a good man. I'm sorry I didn't tell you. I wanted to. But I couldn't. He told me I *couldn't*. It would put you in danger if I told you. I love you, Mama Capra! I love you." Little Jimmy had finally managed to say the words he had wanted to say for years and the ones she longed to hear.

The hearts of The Insiders went out to the boy and his foster mother. Several in the room sniffed and dabbed at tears as the once rambunctious Little

49

Jimmy, whom Mrs. Capra had chased through the children's museum and grocery stores all over town, gently rocked and consoled Mama Capra in his arms. After a while Mrs. Capra pushed LJ gently away and patting his cheek she smiled and whispered, "I'm okay, son. I'm okay. I love you, too." And LJ stood up smiling, still standing by his foster mother's side.

Trying to pick up where he left off, Ron said quietly, "LJ's dad was one of the people who had chased Kat on the mountain…"

And suddenly, just like that, the mood changed again in the room as though someone had thrown the switch. As if they all had suddenly realized that Kat was still missing and they feared something horrible happened to her. The room exploded with shouted questions about Kat's safety and whereabouts. Lenny could be heard above the rest as he bellowed, "Where's my niece?"

Others were shouting, "What about Kat? Is she okay?" "Yes, is Kat okay?" "Where is she?" "We want to know where Kat is?" "Didn't she and Little Jimmy disappear together?" "What happened to her?"

ENTER THE KAT

"I'm here! I've been upstairs listening. I thought it better to stay out of sight. Besides," she said, warmly looking at Little Jimmy, "tonight was all about Jimmy. His night to confront his foes and show his courage… His strength! It was *his night to shine*. He needed to be in charge, and see the ones who have been in control of his life, and who've been out to harm him, feel what he'd been feeling for so long."

As Kat's friends and family surrounded her,

pushing in to hug her, Ron grabbed Baby Ronnie from Kat's arms, grinning from ear to ear, while lifting him up out of their way.

The joy that filled the room was short-lived, when Antoinette asked, *"How could you put us through this?"* The happiness was suddenly replaced by another crash!

The room went silent for a moment but then everyone got angry at the ruse and the trauma they were subjected to. Auntie Antoinette was the loudest, "We were invited here for a—and then *THIS* happened! *What exactly was this?* And why!" The room was again in turmoil, until one powerful voice rose above all others, causing everyone else to be quiet.

"Just wait a minute! This was really a stinking trick to play on us! We were invited to a celebration of life which turned into…. into what?" he repeated what his wife had just said, "What just happened here? And why? I think an explanation is in order!!" Kat's uncle, Sgt. Lenny, shouted, obviously upset. And not just at the ruse, but because he had been kept in the dark.

"Yes!" the angry guests shouted in unison. *"Why?"*

Ron's raised his voice and got everyone's attention. Looking at his wife, he said calmly, "Kat, don't worry, I'm sure your friends will calm down and let you tell your story, but first I want to apologize. As I said earlier, this was mostly my doing. We were under strict orders from Bill Norris, the Chief Investigator for the Attorney General of the State of California, to keep everyone in the dark until a solid investigation was completed," leaving out the

51

well-known fact that he was speaking about his stepfather. "And as for the dual gatherings, how else could I get all the crooks in the county in one place and get them to pay for your lodging at this fine establishment?" The guests looked confused.

Catarina grinned: "Well, they didn't technically 'pay for the rooms.' The rooms were a bonus for the $2500 meals they paid for—and ate." And since they are unable to take advantage of that bonus, you might as well enjoy them." This put smiles on everyone's faces, as they thoroughly enjoyed the joke played on the villains who had caused so much trauma to Kat and Jimmy.

"And now," Catarina announced, "instead of another out-of-hand free-for-all bombardment of questions thrown at LJ and Kat, I thought we could have our own ASK THE RIGHT QUESTION TO GET THE RIGHT ANSWER GAME."

"As much as I hate to override Catarina's game," Ron interrupted, "I must add a few extra rules of my own." His grin widened as he looked at Kat, knowing she was anxious to get down to basics and tell her story. "You are all *insiders*, now. Tonight, you were privy to information about this case that the outsiders don't have yet. Though you've already learned more tonight than you knew this morning, there is much more to learn. This has been a complicated investigation and we're sorry for the… um… *'cat and mouse'* game." No one laughed. Ron coughed and continued, "But we'll let you in on as much as we can tonight. However, there are details you'll have to wait to learn until after the arraignment. We don't want to compromise the case; we've all worked too hard and made too many sacrifices to slip up now."

THE INSIDERS

Ron continued, "You are literally The Insiders… That's the real reason we took all cell phones before the gathering. You must be sequestered until morning at least, at which time I'm sure everything you know will be in the newspaper, since a couple of reporters had been tipped to be here by the… umm… '*former* candidate.'"

Instead of bringing the laughter Ron had hoped for, the room filled once again with shouting questions bombarding the two who had come out of hiding. Through it all, Cassandra, Kat's best friend, had been standing off from the crowd glaring at Kat, angry and hurt for having been put through such horror and worry, But now she made her way through the angry group to face Kat.

THE RIGHT QUESTIONS GET ANSWERS

Kat held Cassandra and the rest of her interrogators at bay, while laying out the ground rules, which were much like the earlier game in the amphitheater, saying, "To get the right answers, the right questions must be asked!" Which didn't set right with The Insiders, who continued shouting demands for answers.

Looking at Cassandra, Kat teased, trying to ward off more daggers being shot her way, "Are you ready to hear the story behind the story? Or are you going to stand there glaring at me?"

Ron put up his palms with pushing motions until everyone finally calmed down, though some of the guests were still murmuring in disappointment.

53

The Game they had all watched being played out on the amphitheater stage had answered many questions, but it had opened up an onslaught of new ones.

To ease the tension, Ron added, "I just spoke with The Chief Investigator for The State of California's Attorney General, Bill Norris." Once again, omitting the fact that he was also Ron's stepdad, "I'm told they're expecting a press conference tomorrow morning, in Sacramento, at which time much of what you've learned tonight will probably be public knowledge, and maybe even more questions will be answered. *But until then,* we need you all to keep anything you've learned among yourselves. And the best way to accomplish that is for you to be guests of Crossroads Inn tonight."

"Yes!" Catarina interjected, eager to get the rowdy Insiders settled in their rooms. "We have rooms for everyone for tonight... and we are *delighted* to have you all as our guests." Seeing the anger ready to erupt again, she added, "But first, perhaps we can persuade Ron to allow a few of your questions to be answered."

Feeling the pressure, Ron said "I'll turn things back over to Kat to answer—*a few questions.*"

What everyone wanted to hear first was how and why Kat and Jimmy had gone into hiding, but Kat only smiled and said, "Lots of groundwork to cover to understand that," which was met with groaning. But Kat was adamant that *"If you want the right answers, ask the right questions,"* putting her hands on her hips imitating Sheriff Buchanan's recognizable stance. This time the joke worked and laughter filled the library, breaking the tension, and soothed nerves that had been unraveling for weeks. Right on cue, servers appeared with platters of hors d'oeuvres, wine, and waters.

As the servers left, the usual sweet and calm Auntie Antoinette demanded angrily, "Why did you and Little Jimmy disappear?"

Momentarily off balance, Kat took a sip of Lake County wine, followed by a deep breath and as briefly as she could tell it, she revealed that Ron had received a false tip that sent him and Jack on a wild goose chase looking for some documents on a hillside near Mare Vista.

"At the very same time," Kat continued, "LJ was leading me to some hidden documents in Mare Vista's tunnel between the barn and house. But we were followed and trapped from both ends of the tunnel. It was a trap set by the very rats who were hired to *kill us both*." Everyone gasped in unison! Kat hurried on, "Ron and Jack were moments away when they were alerted to come to our rescue and make arrests. Little Jimmy consoled me, and led and pushed me into a storm drain leading out the side of the tunnel, and we had to turn off our flashlights. He suddenly had a terrible flashback and anxiety attack. It was too reminiscent of the whole Konocti Caves terror he went through as a kid with that horrible foster dad, Melbourne—or Jones as he called himself then. So it went from him trying to calm and reassure me, to me calming him down. But Ron and Jack arrived in time to trap the rats and at least we were in a safe place to wait until all arrests were made. And with all the noise and shouting in the tunnel no one heard us when we had our breakdowns. Jimmy had been instructed to keep me there until someone came for us, which seemed an eternity, but finally he was given the all clear by Bill Norris to exit the storm drain and head back to my Jeep and wait for Ron. We were told that all of what happened had to be kept under wraps until a thorough investigation could be completed. All the leads and connecting the dots to all who were involved in hiring the hitmen needed to be sorted out and followed to ensure a solid case against…" Kat paused to clear her throat, and regain her composure, as she tried to avoid her aunt's tears and her uncle's glaring eyes. "A solid case against all who were involved with the plot against Jimmy—and myself—needed to be firmly built. Strict *orders from Bill Norris,*" she added.

Then, as The Game in the amphitheater so aptly revealed, the missing documents which seemed to have been found became the focus.

"How did you get your hands on the rest of the documents?" Angel was first to ask.

"*Which* documents?" Kat's Auntie Antoinette interjected.

"Good questions," Ron responded, "Well, there are several documents—some we've known or at least suspected were missing, and some unexpectedly showed up during the last phase of investigations…"

"Please, can you be more specific?" Antionette asked impatiently.

"Okay, so," Ron continued, "you'll remember from The Game in the amphitheater, that James found something in the wall of this library. It was Carolina Jane's second journal. And a handstitched sampler that had hung there for a hundred years, was stolen. While James was prepping the wall to paint, he noticed a loose board and he pulled it off exposing the child's journal.

"That was it?" Mrs. Capra demanded, "A child's diary?"

"No, there's more," Ron said, "and it wasn't *just a child's diary*. It picked up where the first journal left off. It was started when Carolina Jane was a child but she wrote in it up until she was an adult. Finding it is how we learned that she escaped her kidnappers and recovered from amnesia, which was of personal interest to us; but it also held some key pieces to the puzzle Kat had been trying to put together..."

"I thought you said documents were found," Antoinette interrupted.

"Yes, well okay," Ron began again, "well Sal, who as we all know now, had been a turncoat, giving the perps any information he overheard, or uncovered..." Sal was standing off a bit from the others and hung his head as his wife, who was standing on the other side of the group as far from him as she could get, looked at him with distain.

"Well," Ron continued explaining, "When James left to take the journal to Catarina and Eduardo, Sal checked out the wall and found more of the missing documents, letters, and journals, which over the century and a half of Lake County earthquakes, had fallen deeper into the wall. He pulled them out, and quickly stashed them under a paint tarp, planning to give them to Johnny Amoretti later. But later that night, when he retrieved them and looked them over, it struck him that the information he'd just uncovered, could cause his wife's family to lose the inn. Crossroads Inn. Sal knew how much it

57

meant to them all... and only at that moment did he realize how much the Spidiacci family meant to him. He could suddenly see clearly that the crooks had only befriended him to use him. Johnny had lied to him about their plans involving only the mountain. Now he saw they were after Crossroads Inn Time B&B and Spa, too… the very thing that tied the Spidiacci's, Tess, and him, as well as James, all together. Sal felt ashamed. But there was something else. As he read Sam's journal and other documents, he began to be afraid of the more dangerous ramifications of the Spears' connection with Crossroads. What at first seemed like a great historic connection that could be marketed, was now the means of his family *losing* not only their home and business, but quite possibly their lives. After speaking with the Spidiacci's, Sal cornered me the next time he could get me alone and passed me a note asking to meet with him. When we met up, he told me what he'd found and gave me the documents and said he kept them at first because he just couldn't let that happen to his family, but he knew what he had to do and his in-laws agreed. He confessed that he'd allowed himself to be suckered into being used by Johnny Amoretti for information. He wanted to make it up to me, but especially his wife and family, even though he knew it was dangerous.

"I arranged a secret meeting with Sal and Jack. After that he answered directly to Jack; and Sal agreed to carry on as a mole to gather intel about Johnny Amoretti, Lois Kipper, and Linda—who it has been discovered were using assumed identities, hiding the fact that Lois is married to Johnny Amoretti and Linda is their daughter. And the apple

58

didn't fall far from the tree. Linda had been legal secretary for Steven Pinero. And several years ago she accompanied Pinero when he got on the plane with the mob's money, along with his wife Theo Pinero's Trust Fund. Reportedly, Pinero was met in Italy by the mob's hitman, Enzo. Well, as it turns out the man that exited the plane was someone Pinero set up to be his double, so he was the one who was met and left with Enzo, never to be seen again. As for Linda, she took the next flight back and talked her way back into working for the same law firm and is now Eugene Smith's legal secretary and *girlfriend*."

"Who is actually the real *Pinero*!" Lenny guessed gruffly, not wanting to join in, due to being left out of the loop, but it just slipped out.

"Exactly!" Ron said in Lenny's direction. "Anyway, from then on Sal only gave Johnny information that Jack told him to. Most of which would be misinformation. And as time went on, he agreed to try to get in deeper with them, to keep us informed as to their plans and whereabouts. Sal even became Johnny's go-to guy... otherwise known as 'gopher' or '*flunky*'." Ron glanced at Tess, and was relieved to see the sympathetic expression he'd hoped for, as she looked at her husband. "There's hope for them," Ron thought, as he met Kat's eyes, who gave him a small grateful smile to let him know she knew he wasn't just being mean by putting Sal down. Kat had been worried about her friend Tess's marriage. But seeing Tess's expression gave her hope.

Ron grinned at Sal and continued, "Sal has been an *integral* part in this investigation. With his help, we were able to set the stage for several intriguing reversal of plots meant to beat us in finding certain documents and clues, or to trap us. Sal has not only been a great help, but has shown *real courage* in some *pretty stressful* situations, with some *extremely dangerous* individuals." Looking at Tess, he said, "You have good reason to be proud of your man." Tess, who had obviously known her husband had been keeping things from her, and spending more time than ever away from the inn, had been worried about their marriage. Although she smiled, it was obvious Sal had a lot of explaining to do. Tess was not only upset at her husband; it was clear her mother and father were privy to how Sal had fit into *'The Game.'* Not only that, they had actually kept the entire investigation from her. She knew something was going on, but had no idea there were *criminals* staying at the inn, or that her husband was involved with them *in any way*.

"Am I that dense?" Tess wondered aloud. "How could all this be happening around me, without my having a clue?"

Catarina looked sadly at her daughter. She knew there would be much needed work to heal this breach in what her daughter viewed as deceit. It wasn't out of malice or distrust that she withheld information from her daughter concerning her husband. It was out of *concern for her safety*. Catarina had been afraid that her daughter wouldn't be able to conceal what she knew, or her thoughts and feelings about the scoundrels her husband was being 'friendly' with—which could put her in real danger. And Tess' reaction to learning of Sal's one-time disloyalty to the family, and how evident it was that she was feeling sorry for Sal when it seemed Ron was belittling him, gave evidence that it was the correct decision not to bring Tess in on 'The Game'. Her reactions and facial expressions made her an open book.

But now, seeing Tess' pain in being left out of the loop and being treated like a child, made Catarina's heart ache. She longed to go comfort her, but she knew it was Sal's place to do that. That would be the first step toward healing their differences. Although she had always had her doubts about him, after the way he humbled himself to be Johnny's flunky, as Ron put it, to gain information to help with the investigation, and considering his motives for hiding the documents to protect the *family*,well, Catarina couldn't be prouder or love her son-in-law more.

Tears suddenly filled Catarina's eyes at the thought of losing her beloved Victorian inn. But she knew it would probably soon be a reality she would have to face. There was in fact a Spears heir-apparent in their midst tonight. She turned to hide her emotions, but her teary eyes met with Ron's.

"But, Kat! Won't you now, *please,* tell us where you've been, and why you didn't let me know! You had better have a good reason for scaring us all half to de..." halting and covering her mouth not able to even say the word, Cassandra Anna Marie Locascio began to sob.

Kat hugged her childhood friend, , who was now flaunting a large diamond engagement ring, and teased, "As much as I'd like to, I can't tell you any more. You heard the rules: to get the right answer, ask the *right question.*" Tears still on her cheeks Cassandra rolled her eyes. Her fiancé Jack Moran, the private detective, and onetime confirmed bachelor, stepped up to her rescue.

Leaning close to her, he whispered a suggestion in her ear.

"Hey! No fair! *No inside information!*" shouted Angel.

"That's right! Besides," Lenny chimed in gruffly, "I think there are a few details we need to clear up before we go *there*."

"You're right, Uncle Lenny. But first, I have a question of my own," and hoping to lighten the mood again while distracting her uncle, Kat looked sternly at her friend, "for *Miss* Locascio!" she said, pretending to scold. "Just how is it that my best friend and bridesmaid has had an entire courtship right under my nose, without saying a word? And just why have I been denied the privilege of hostessing your engagement party?"

Looking at Jack, who was clearly blushing, Cassandra said coyly, "Well, that is a long story. One I think that we'll hold onto for a while."

"Ah-hmm!" grunted Ron, stepping up to take the spotlight off his friend and further distract his boss, Lenny.

THE PLAN

"Little Jimmy gets the credit—or blame—depending how ya look at it, for his and Kat's escape," Ron chuckled. "He and his dad planned the whole wild goose—or document—thing up with Jack and Bill Norris because the perps were closing in on him and Kat and frankly, *he was scared*. Who wouldn't be if they had half a dozen known criminals plotting their demise?" Ron waited as the crowd gasped, and exchanged wide-eyed glances at each other, followed by widespread mumbling. The seriousness of the situation was finally sinking in.

"So, jumping to the tail end of the story—the part I'm sure you all want to hear. Little Jimmy had Jack call Lenny and myself to go with him to two locations, one local and the other out of county. Lenny stayed in Lake County, while Jack drove me just above Mare Vista, in the Santa Cruz Mountains, off a fire trail, saying he'd received a tip about the missing documents. Putting us there just ahead of Kat, Jimmy, and the *hitmen*. So, when I got the call about Kat and Jimmy being trapped in the tunnel, Jack and I would be just moments from Mare Vista, to close in at each end of the tunnel to rescue Kat and Jimmy... and capture the hired thugs. Hitmen!" Ron paused briefly to clear his throat, "Jimmy and his dad had studied the Mare Vista's blueprints and knew of the storm drainage off the tunnel. They had explored it on one of their excursions to Mare Vista to make sure it was safe and not blocked. Jimmy's dad is not much larger than Kat. But when Kat and Jimmy ducked into the drainage tunnel Jimmy knew it was too tight for the thugs... and after the thugs were taken into custody, a text was sent from their cell phone 'caught the pests in the trap, and took care of them. Heading back to our fishing trip,' as if they were establishing an alibi." Ron knew he was repeating what was said earlier but he knew Kat had spoken so fast, some may still have questions and besides, the more he talked about what they had already heard, the less time they would have to drill him about information that was off-limits.

"Kat and Jimmy exited from the other end of the drainage tunnel and I met them at her Jeep and drove them home, while Jack called Lenny and said it looked like a hoax tip and we should all go home."

Kat, who never missed an opportunity to tell a good story, and seeing the anger on her uncle's face for being left out of the loop, jumped in and began telling how Jimmy had led her to where she thought she was going to find the final piece of the puzzle. Instead they were trapped in Mare Vista's tunnel from each end and barely escaped through a drainage vent, just as Ron showed up to capture the rats who were caught in their own trap. "By the time Ron was reading them their rights, Jimmy and I were safely in the back seat of my Jeep." Pausing to give Jimmy a teasing look, Kat continued, "Where Jimmy pleaded for my forgiveness."

Jimmy cut in, "I never meant to scare you Kat. My Waa… Uhh… *my father* thought if you knew the plan, you wouldn't come with me. And I *had to rescue you*. They were planning to…" Little Jimmy's voice choked.

Ron interrupted with, "When the thugs were in custody, facing attempted murder, they were given the choice to turn in state's evidence or life in prison—they chose wisely. And with everyone thinking that Kat and LJ were *out of the picture*, all the bad guys relaxed and moved forward with their evil plans; so, when invitations were sent out saying there was a big announcement for Fumaroles' future, they all thought it was a celebration announcement and they all gladly paid the $2500 per plate ticket."

Lenny motioned to Ron and opened his mouth, but just as he was about to renew his complaint, Cassandra interrupted, "*But where were you all this time?*" not wanting to hear any more of the terrible fate her best friend had been rescued from.

"We were right under your nose!" Kat said, again with hands on hips. "Turnabout is fair play!" she laughed. "To be exact, we were at Ron's and *my house*.

"It was a bit tricky for Jimmy and I to sneak inside, since so many people were watching the house. LJ had ridden in the cargo area of the Jeep and I was on the floorboard behind the front seats. Ron parked in the garage, and walked into the house. Since Angel was already at our house, because she and Mom were watching Baby Ronnie, Ron told her to put on a hat and go the garage. We exchanged clothing and I grabbed her hat and walked quickly inside dressed like Angel, while she and LJ crawled through the crawl space from the garage and climbed down through the trap door in the closet. Glad I didn't have to do that!" Kat said, "But I did have to lay on the floor behind the seat for a long time." She pouted making everyone laugh again.

Ron interjected, "To be clear, we weren't concerned about anyone bugging the house. After the Konocti Caves incident, we had a scrambler installed that will mess up any listening device. The hard part was keeping Kat and Jimmy out of sight during the rest of the investigation. They spent most of their days downstairs in the family room and office. Jimmy camped out on my office floor, where he was perfectly happy having a computer at his disposal 24/7.

"And of course, Kat was deliriously happy being able to spend so much time with Baby Ronnie. Since Caroline and Angel were still staying at our house to help with Ronnie, and to keep the ruse going, Angel and Kat dressed alike and were careful to not be near a window at the same time.

"And between the three of them, Kat, LJ, and… his dad, they continued to monitor the entire long list of perps' movements and plans. Jimmy and his dad took the chart Kat had started and in no time had figured out the family and criminal connections, and tied everyone together, noting where their plots overlapped.

Mrs. Capra blurted loudly, "That's what I want to know! Where has Jimmy's dad been all these years?" And looking at Ron and Kat, she frowned, "And how long have you two known about him?" It was obvious she suspected something and was not going to be ignored or distracted.

Kat smiled, and raising her brows, looked at Ron who nodded, "Ron told you previously didn't he, about Little Jimmy's ride-along? Well, that's when Jimmy told Ron he was scared the Lombardis had evil plans for him. All the other foster brothers had either aged out of the system, were sent to prep school, college, or boarding schools, or adopted, etc. Jimmy was left there alone. With two more years of high school and no plan or even talk of the future."

In unison everyone said, "*Oh no!*"

And then Mrs. Capra said sternly, "Ron never told us about Little Jimmy's *ride-along*!"

Ron grinned and said, "Well, if I can get a word in," and then winked at Kat before beginning to explain that Jimmy had showed up at his work early one morning and he took him for a ride-along in his patrol car and told him about meeting someone on the mountain.

LJ piped in with, "Yeah, I told him about

meeting someone on the mountain who had been watching me but seeing Ron's clenched jaw, I told him not to worry. He's harmless. Just a little strange, I admitted." At this, LJ laughed out loud, but the guests looked at each other, not getting the joke. "And I told Ron I trusted him," LJ continued, "and like I told you all earlier, I met him on the mountain one day when I was hiking to the top of Mount Hannah. He said he knew my mother. He told me things about her. And he knew a lot about me."

It was Ron's turn to interrupt, "It was getting more difficult to stay calm and just listen but I knew I must, or Jimmy would clam up. All my instincts were to find this creep and make sure he stayed far away from Jimmy. When Jimmy said, the guy was his…"

Jimmy interjected, "My *Watcher*, that's what he called himself at first, he said he'd been watching over me since my mother died."

Ron cut in again, "Yeah, I seriously nearly lost it at that! That is until Jimmy said, '*The Watcher* couldn't help him in this situation, and that *The Watcher* suggested he *talk to me*.' That's when I stopped talking and listened."

Jimmy again interrupted and said; "Yeah, he said to prove he was on the up-and-up, tell Ron that he was the one who changed my background record on Ron and Kat's computers, so they would know that I was in danger. And he changed them back after he knew they'd seen it. He said, then Ron would know he was on the square. I told Ron that The Watcher had been following Kat, because I said he should try to talk to her. But he said there were too many surveillance cameras to try anywhere except on one side of Cobb Mountain. I told Ron there were lots of cameras where he and Jack had been searching for… well… searching for clues. I asked Ron if he knew they'd been watching them, but right then I got a text from The Watcher and he told me he had a plan and to stop talking and meet up with him. So, I told Ron we better wait about saying anything to anyone because I might have been wrong about something, and then asked to be dropped off at school. I told him to not say anything to anyone—especially not Kat—because The Watcher had come up with a plan." Jimmy's voice trailed off, and for the first time that night his face revealed just how vulnerable he felt.

Ron picked up his story and continued, "And that was the last I saw Jimmy until leaving Mare Vista after the arrests. The drive home is when Jimmy told me more about The Watcher. He said he had been a recluse since the war, but was a skilled computer hacker, and that's how he had traced his fiancée, but was too late. She had died. But when he found out about their baby, he didn't quit until he found him."

Little Jimmy suddenly stood up. He looked like he wanted to say something but was afraid he would get too emotional. The room was silent and all eyes were on him. He once again took a deep breath and began talking.

"He started telling me about his son. How smart he was and how proud he made him. And how he knew his son was stronger than he thought he was. He told me all the things his son liked to do and the high grades he got in school. The more he told me about his son, the more I suspected he was talking about..." LJ stopped, looking down at the floor. The room was still quiet. When Jimmy looked up all he saw were smiling faces with teary eyes.

"*Me!*" Jimmy said gleefully. "He was talking about me, and he was proud I was *his son*." His voice cracked and he had to regain his composure. Little Jimmy finally piped up again, with a smile, "And he had been watching over me, hacking into computers and emails of everyone around me. I know that sounds sorta bad, but he knew I was in danger. He told me only to trust Kat and Ron—and Mrs. Capra," Little Jimmy looked at her with such love in his eyes before continuing, "And Dr. Fleming—but said to *be careful around him*, because he was surrounded by bad people. He said that everyone had alternative plans that could mean bad things for me.

"My dad had gotten odd jobs all around the county. Mostly night jobs where he hacked into computers and found out about some seriously dangerous things going on. He told me about some of the things, and helped me cope and to stay clear of danger. He also taught me how to hack computers," LJ added nonchalantly. "We hacked into Kat's home computer to follow her investigation, and then Kat's and Ron's work computers just to let them know who I really was. My real name. So they would know I was in dire danger. We quickly deleted the information after Kat made a print out."

Jimmy looked down, not wanting to show just how scared he felt. "I felt trapped. Just like when Kat and I were in the tunnel. And I was desperate to get out of the Lombardis' custody, but knew I couldn't go to the police, because everyone in the county thought the Lombardi's were great people, and I should be grateful for them taking in a poor orphan like me." Pausing to gain control again, LJ said strongly, "And without proof... proof obtained *legally*, and with warrants to search computers, and homes, there was no probable cause. And no one could legally open their home to me because... basically I belong to the state. If I ran away, I'd end up homeless, with no future... and I seriously wanted to finish school. I want to do things... *good things* with my life. To make a difference. Especially with ecology. Dad urged me to talk Ron into talking to his stepdad, Bill Norris. That's why I rode my bike that morning and asked Ron for a ride-along, so I could ask him to get Bill Norris to call me. But just when I was about to, Dad called and said he thought of a plan and not to say anything more to Ron.

"It was Dad's plan to lure everyone to Mare Vista… he would set the thing up… timed it out… for Ron and Jack to already be near Mare Vista when I took Kat there. We knew the perps had planted a device on her car and they would follow. Dad said if Ron knew the plan, he wouldn't let Kat go. So, he called Bill Norris… well he contacted him. Okay… he hacked into his computer to tell him." That surprised, shocked, and then filled the room with laughter. Much needed laughter. No one was laughing as loudly as Little Jimmy.

When the laughter calmed down, Ron said proudly, "But even before Jimmy's dad came into the picture, Kat figured out that LJ was a direct bloodline to The Fumaroles…" Jimmy turned to look straight at Ron, lifting one eyebrow. Ron flushed, suddenly realizing Kat only found out because things showed up on her computer. "Okay, he was already in the

70

picture... but I didn't know it yet... I guess he was always in the background, leading us. Leaving clues on our computers..." then realizing what he'd revealed he added, "Yeah, that's right— he hacked my computer. He's a hacker, like LJ said. The best I've ever seen. So good, in fact, that Bill Norris has arranged amnesty for him in exchange for his services."

The room was quiet for a few moments and Little Jimmy's face, though looking down at his hands, was bright red. He knew all eyes were on him. He couldn't help feeling that they all still thought of him as the little troublemaker running around the children's museum, causing havoc, and still blamed him for what happened to his friends in the mine. And now they probably thought he would hack their computers.

Kat shot Angel a worried look and spoke out, trying to get the attention off the boy by asking, "What did Catarina mean earlier when she said there's an heir to Crossroads Inn Time, Ron?" Having picked up on Kat's worried expression, Angel agreed, "I was wondering that, too!"

It worked, because others piped in wanting answers to that question.

Relieved to have Little Jimmy removed from an uncomfortable situation, Ron laughed—a little too loud—and said, "All in due time. But you're forgetting the rules to this game."

That did it, the room was filled with loud debates over how the questions should have been asked, giving Little Jimmy time to slip out of the room and onto the veranda where Bill Norris was waiting to take him into protective custody.

Kat watched as the tail lights disappeared down the driveway, and sighed with relief. She knew that although most of the perps were in custody, LJ was still in jeopardy. Perhaps by one—or more—in the room right now.

Ron kept the attention of everyone by saying, "Alright, alright! I'll answer that question. But not tonight. That answer would take all night, and Kat and I need to get our baby home and into his own bed." Grandma Caroline entered the room carrying the little bundle of joy to his mommy. As Ron and Kat left, Catarina announced, "Yes, it is getting late. I have your rooms made up and ready for you all tonight... since it seems all my prepaid bookings have been abruptly canceled," and this time it created laughter to fill the room. "Ron and Kat will be back in the morning to finish their story. If you'll stop by the front desk, your keys will be given to you."

The guests couldn't help but notice there were still plenty of FBI men on the premises.

CHAPTER FOUR

EVERYONE'S GOT A STORY
BUT NOT EVERYONE'S A GOOD ONE

EXTRA "B" IN B&B.... BEST BREAKFAST

Crossroads Inn's guests were allowed to sleep until 7:00 a.m., at which time they all received a wakeup call and invitation to a buffet breakfast in the library at 8:00 a.m. They were told that coffee or tea could be brought to their rooms earlier if they wished.

Anticipating her guests would be anxious to hear the rest of Kat and Jimmy's story, and the investigation conclusion that led to last night's 'Reveal' and arrests, Catarina had a delicious breakfast buffet already set and waiting to greet them as they entered the library.

Never missing the detail that makes a meal special, Kat had designed a welcoming tablescape and arranged it herself. A side bar held carafes of hot coffee and hot water, a basket filled with multiple choices of teas and hot chocolate, and glass pitchers of mimosa. Two cheerful and bright floral arrangements were perched high on pillars framing the chafing dishes and platters arranged beautifully yet functionally, ready to serve up Catarina's classic breakfast buffet consisting of two platters of fresh fruit with apple-date dip, fluffy zucchini frittata made from Mama DeCanti's recipe, which she gave Catarina personally, specialty ground Italian breakfast sausage from the Lucerne Lakeview Market's national award-winning butcher, and cottage potatoes with secret seasoning only Chef

Salvatore knows; hot from the oven, bake 'n serve apple cinnamon crescents from Marcel's French Bakery just up the highway in Clearlake Oaks, which Catarina kept a freezer shelf reserved for; and apple fritters and fresh baked sourdough baguettes that James picked up, also from Marcel's no more than fifteen minutes before the first guest began descending into the library, speculating on the new information they would learn about The Fumaroles on Cobb Mountain and all the *fat cat investors* and scoundrels who had been living among them. Some guests were more anxious than others. A few were not anxious at all.

You would think that all the food consumed the night before would have lasted the *Insiders* a while longer, but the aroma of fresh brewed coffee, Italian sausage, frittata, and baked bread floating up the stairs, had them lined up at the buffet table right on time. John Buchanan was the first to join Catarina and Eduardo in the library and they were shortly joined by Dr. Richard Fleming, who walked in with Jack Moran, who had worked part time for the doctor before his private detective agency took off. The two were in the middle of a lively conversation about a new program the doctor would soon be offering at the retreat. However, Jack was soon distracted by the arrival of his fiancée, Cassandra Locascio and Kat's little sister, Angel. Dr. Fleming smiled and with a knowing nod he turned and began chatting with Eduardo. James and his sister, Theo, walked in together smiling, but after filling a plate from the buffet they walked away in opposite directions to sit with different groups of people.

Theo was ecstatic to find out that her ex-husband was going to get his comeuppance and even more interested in finding out in what bank her trust money had been gaining interest. Other than that, Theo was more eager to catch up with Lydia than hear more about The Fumaroles and vendettas. Though they spoke with each other as well as the four other women who all met at Crossroads several years ago, she hadn't seen Lydia in a while.

James pulled up a chair next to Sal and Tess. The room was soon abuzz with conversation as the guests milled around the buffet, some not bothering to take a seat as they joined one huddled group conversing excitedly with theories or questions before moving on to the next group and then to the next, joining in the conversation of each before finally finding a seat or heading back to the buffet.

As Ron and Kat entered the room, all eyes clung to Kat as she filled a plate from the buffet and found a chair and began to eat, not making eye contact with anyone. They were the only ones in the library who did not spend the night at the inn. Ron filled his plate and leaned on the wall protectively next to his wife. Though he didn't speak, his body language loudly proclaimed no rude or angry comments will be tolerated. Soon, low murmurs could be heard from each group, but no one pressed Kat for answers to their many unanswered questions.

INSIDER'S GAME

When all in the library had visited the buffet table at least once, Catarina stood and invited everyone to give their attention to Kat, who would continue answering questions where they left off the night before.

Kat stood preparing to speak to the eager group gathered. The previous evening ended rather abruptly and they woke up hungry for more than food! The more than a dozen sequestered guests were hungry for more details and answers that they were silently demanding to hear. Kat's eyes slowly went around the room, lingering on some, skimming over others.

All eyes were on her as she began with: "Good morning, I trust you all slept well," she smiled, "I want to thank Catarina and Eduardo again for their fine hospitality. I'm sure you agree that Crossroads puts one more B in B&B… Best Breakfast!" After the nods ended and chuckles quieted down, she got right down to business—or rather didn't get down to business, "Actually… I'm afraid this morning we are not going to pick up where we left off last night. We've got good news and we've got—not really bad news. There are still things being sorted out in Sacramento, making it imperative that we keep the lid on a bit tighter and a bit longer than we'd anticipated."

This brought a loud unison groan of disappointment from the guests of Crossroads Inn Time B&B and Spa, which would be the last thing everyone in the room would agree on for some time.

"Now for some good news." Kat interrupted the groans. "Crossroads Inn Time's hospitality has been extended by request of the State of California, who is picking up the bill." This bit of news brought silence from some, murmurs from many, and a few groans. As the ramifications of being further sequestered sank in, the groanings grew in numbers and volume.

"This is all very nice, and I don't want to sound ungrateful, but I really want to *go home*!" Antoinette complained. "How long are we going to be kept here?"

Catarina stood up, smiled her famous drop-dead gorgeous smile, and cleared her throat. Picking up a Mimosa, she tapped it with a butter knife, which got everyone's attention and brought all eyes back on her.

With her famous smile Catarina let her sparkling blue eyes roam the room, searching the faces and body languages of her guests. Beginning in an almost hushed voice she said, "In my experience running this B&B and Spa—the many groups and counseling sessions I've directed and sat in on—I've learned an undeniable truth: Everyone has a story to tell" and raising one eyebrow she added, "but not everyone has a good one, and some... well, some may not even realize they actually do have a story. Sometimes it takes a bit of work... a bit of patience to get to the heart of their story. Hmmm yes. Heart. All stories begin and end with the heart. As with last night, to get the right answer you *must ask the right question*. We just can't ask the right questions now. But..."

"As a matter of fact," Ron interrupted, "not surprising there has been an influx of big-named attorneys descending upon this community—injunctions in hand—to stop any such questions from being discussed. They are already working hard to tangle things up so tightly, it will no doubt take a while to sort it all out. Not as long as they are hoping, but a while." Again, the groans and murmuring filled the library.

Undeterred, Catarina smiled and continued, "Now, although, as Kat and Ron explained, we won't be discussing the huge case being sorted out today—apparently not even most of what we heard last night—but we did learn a lot last night about the major perpetrators of the case."

Kat's uncle, Sergeant Lenard, interrupted her gruffly, "Actually we only learned enough to have even more questions!" This brought more groans and murmuring.

"I know, I know," Catarina said over the voices, "But we need to set it all aside for just a bit. We've been asked not to discuss it anymore for the time being. But that doesn't mean we don't have things we can discuss! All those old journals and letters, for instance. Some *pretty juicy stuff* there. Things that affect people in this room even now, all these years later.

"Not only that but here in this room," Catarina lifted her eyebrows, "right here... right now... there are so many mysteries to be solved." Catarina paused to give a mischievous smile. "We all know each other, some more than others, but there are things about each of us that we don't know, but perhaps wonder about. I understand many—or most—of you have had the pleasant experience over the past couple months of joining officer Ron Simmons on what is called a 'ride-along' during which time you had the most pleasant conversations. Some of you were able to figure out things you'd been wondering about; others may have realized they knew things about the goings on of our fair county that they hadn't realized they knew. Some left their ride-along not knowing they had helped the case Ron

78

and Kat had been trying to unravel for years. Others may have tried hard to keep secrets concealed that they've been hiding for well, perhaps decades..." Catarina's sparkling eyes sparkled even more as she said, "Secrets that some of us here today perhaps have suspected or wondered about. Kat and I thought that as long as we steer it in a bit of a different direction, a little more of a game of ASK RIGHT, TELL ALL could be not only fun, but perhaps informative. Some of us may not realize that the information we have could perhaps be of a great benefit for others... others right here in this room."

This sparked enthusiasm in the room, for the most part. Though there were still some jaws clenched and lips tightened. And some looked like they were bursting at the seams to spill their beans!

With a laugh in her voice, Catarina declared, "Everyone will have a chance to ask questions or tell their story of discovery... or how they are involved, or their suspicions, or what they heard, know, or saw. But first...

THE GAME BY ANY OTHER NAME IS STILL THE GAME

"Okay, I'll start," began Angel, who was one of the 'sequestered' guests. "I'll ask the first question. Although Mom and I knew you and LJ were downstairs this whole time, and we had been privy to some of the mysteries and investigations prior to your *disappearance*, I never knew until last night that James was involved somehow in all this..." Then looking boldly at James, she asked, "So! It was *you* who cut the missing pages out of Carolina Jane's journal. What was that all about? Are you or were

79

you in cahoots with the bad guys?"

"Wait!" Auntie Antoinette blurted, "You were hiding out in your home this entire time? Why didn't you let *me* know?" Tears began running down her cheeks. "I was worried sick!" She obviously got over the shock of her niece showing up after such a long period of being missing, but was now dwelling on the fact that she and Lenny were out of the loop. Unable to keep speaking but clearly upset, she turned to her husband, who had also spent the night at the inn and was more angry than hurt. Lenny hugged Antoinette consolingly and glared at his nieces. Kat winced. She had never been the recipient of Lenny's notorious glare before. She feared she'd see it more before the day was over.

Angel gave her aunt a pleading look, "I'm so sorry Auntie. I didn't want to deceive you. But it was necessary for everyone's safety that people thought she was…" Angel couldn't bring herself to say the word. Her uncle didn't like to be kept in the dark about anything, but especially where his nieces were concerned. Having no kids of his own, he stepped in after their father had been killed in an accident, and did his best to provide a father figure to his sister's daughters.

Avoiding looking at Lenny, Ron took it from there, "Yes, Kat and LJ have been hiding in our home on Edgewater. Under everyone's noses. Only myself, LJ's dad, Bill Norris, Caroline, and Angel knew Kat and LJ's whereabouts. Since everyone was either under a shadow of suspicion or perhaps being watched themselves, even Antoinette and Lenny were kept in the dark. If you didn't know anything, there was nothing to hide.

"When I drove Kat's Jeep home, they were in the back, Jimmy lying down under covers in the cargo area, and Kat on the floor behind the driver's seat. A precaution that was probably overly cautious, since the perps thought they had been *'taken care of.'* But just in case not all the perps got the memo and were still watching the house, we decided to err on the side of caution. Jimmy stayed out of sight, in the office, which he loved, since he had use of the computer 24/7."

"And Kat and I," Angel piped up, "could never be out in the open in the same room—or near a window or on the deck at the same time, in case someone spied on us with a telescope.

"And so, Kat's been hiding in plain sight pretending to be me," Angel laughingly said, "dressing and acting like me, which was pretty funny. Ron opened up closets downstairs to connect to each other and to the office, so Kat could move around undetected. And I could duck out of sight so Kat could take care of her baby."

Seeing Antoinette's eyes tear up, Kat quickly added, "Ron and I only found out after the fact that this had all been pre-planned by Little Jimmy and his dad, with the blessings of the California State Attorney General, who was pleased as punch when he got word *exactly which perp,* they now had the goods on. In the meantime, Jimmy continued his schooling via the Internet, and I was happy as could be to be safely home with both *my sons.*

"And to continue the ruse, Mom and Angel 'moved in' supposedly to console Ron, and to help care for the baby. Which gave me plenty of time to tidy up loose ends in the investigation, and to help

Jimmy come up with the 'questions' for the reveal party—*both of them*—the amphitheater ruse to put the perps in jail, and the gathering in the library to let all who cared know that Jimmy and I were safe, in such a way that by the end of the evening, they would thank us for including them in the ruse. Well... almost." She laughed nervously, trying to avoid her aunt and uncle's eyes.

Seeing her aunt's pained expression, Angel winced and added quickly, "Kat & Little Jimmy were holed up in the house with only the Internet to continue their investigation... Kat kept barking orders at Jack and Ron while taking orders from LJ's dad," hoping to add some humor, "Boy! Did she have everyone jumping!"

Ron interjected, "Little Jimmy came up with the brilliant way to interview witnesses without drawing any suspicions from superiors who were definitely *suspect*s and needed to be kept in the dark; and even those being interviewed had no idea they were either suspects or may have had useful information."

JIMMY'S PLAN

After a pause Ron almost reluctantly said, "Some of you may remember being part of a ride-along program sponsored by the county." Then, clearing his throat and standing up straighter and in forced confident voice, added, "Well, Jimmy had instructed me to suggest to Lenny that he might initiate a ride-along PR campaign to improve public opinion of the department. Lenny agreed as long as I would be the one giving the rides, which worked out perfectly. The high sheriff approved of the project, no doubt thinking it would be great PR for himself and his campaign; while also keeping Lenny and me busy and out of the business of investigating issues 'above our pay grade.' Ron laughed nervously at the shocked faces staring back at him.

"I typed up and made copies of unsolicited ride-along invitations," Ron continued, "and Lenny sent them out to who he thought were random Lake County residents. Some *were* random; however, some were selected by LJ's dad." Ron diverted his eyes from another glare shot his way by his boss.

"While waiting for responses," Kat picked up where Ron left off, "Dr. Fleming coached and helped Ron hone skills he already possessed—that of interviewing and getting people to say more than they intended to say. Ron was instructed to just start a conversation and let them talk. Adding to what they said, here and there, thereby bringing out truths that they may have not been aware they knew. Some of the invited individuals had no idea they had helpful information for an ongoing investigation. However, if they disclosed something of interest, they were later called into a secret Grand Jury to testify and sworn to secrecy. But they had no idea who else were also being called in to testify. Some, however, knew exactly that they needed to hide facts and distort truths, to conceal what they knew only too well were things Ron would very much like to know. Ron was taught what body language revealed that someone was holding something back, or lying." While Kat spoke, Ron was taking particular interest in the expressions and nervous movements of some of the listeners. One, in particular, caught Kat's attention.

RED HERRINGS OR SNAKES IN THE GRASS?

Auntie Antoinette was the first to speak up. "We were a bit suspicious of Catarina and Eduardo but...", apparently deciding if 'you can't lick them join them', "...well, it's pretty obvious, since they.... since *we are all here*, not in jail, *none of us* were involved! And it's obvious that Cat and Eduardo, the owners of Crossroads Inn, were not connected to any of this, otherwise they, *and we*, wouldn't be *here*."

Ron agreed and replied, "You're right about Catarina and Eduardo. They have been very helpful in our investigation. Though they *did* have to play up to the perps a bit, to gain their trust in coming to the event... yeah, they have been very helpful. They had a lot to lose, too. But they're honest people. And I do need to correct you on one thing. The fact that we are all here doesn't mean none of us could be involved," Ron said nonchalantly but pausing to see what expressions that statement might cause before going on. "Some here may be involved without knowing it."

Catarina got things back on track with: "So back to Angel's question. James care to answer?"

"Yes," agreed Caroline, "What was that question that tripped up James at the Reveal Party?" Angel choked on the juice she had just taken a sip of, and burst out laughing. Other snickers could be heard around the room at Caroline's unintentional pun. Caroline looked confused, but asked, "Who found what in the wall? And why did James cut pages out of a journal?"

"When I was repairing the wall," replied a red-faced James, who was clearly uncomfortable by the way Caroline worded her question due to his limp, even though he knew that Caroline would never be that cruel. "I found an old journal written by Carolina Jane," he clarified further, "the niece of the man who built Crossroads. It was just a stagecoach stop back then when it was first built. I knew Kat was anxious to find it, because it was Carolina Jane's second journal, and there was so much left hanging in the first. So, I was on the way to find Catarina to give it to her and Eduardo so they could take it to Kat, but I couldn't resist taking a peek. What I read disturbed me. I was afraid, and rightly so, that it would cause Catarina and Eduardo to have to forfeit the inn. Sal knew I found the journal, so I knew I had to turn it over to my sister, but I cut the damning pages out. But Catarina can read me like a book, and knew right away I was hiding something. I finally fessed up and she insisted I give the pages to Kat… which I did."

Kat added, "James and Catarina were both caught off-guard last night, when Jimmy called into question James' loyalty and motivations. But that was just to let the perps know how widely-read the documents were, and that they had already been turned over to the right people, in case they thought they could still get their hands on them. They are useless to anyone but the rightful heir now.

"Wait! I thought it was you, Sal, that found it. Didn't you find a journal or something that could cause Catarina to lose Crossroads?" Angel demanded.

"Yes," Cassandra chimed in, "didn't you find something in the wall too, Sal?" Sal just nodded, still feeling guilty.

"Yes, Cassandra and Angel, you're both

right," Kat said quickly, wanting to squelch this question quickly and not put Sal through the grinder again. "While James left with the journal he found, Sal found some of the other missing journals, documents, and letters and stashed them until he could retrieve them and take a look. He was planning on selling them to Johnny Amaretti until he started reading them and realized what they meant. And later he read Carolina Jane's final entries and realized the ramifications of the wrong people getting their hands on the journal. And he feared for his family's inn, the same way James did. They had the same good motive, just bad reactions to them. In Sal's case, he stashed the journals and documents to give him time to think it over. In the end, both Sal and James came forth, and everything was turned over to Ron.

"James and Sal were both worried about their family losing what brought them all together and they all worked hard to build—especially Catarina. She had put her heart into the inn and was now faced with the fact that Crossroads Inn Time Bed and Breakfast legally and rightfully belonged to someone else." Kat was anxious that everyone in the library understood that James, Sal and Catarina were all good people. People with flaws, yes, and like everyone, they worried about their families. And that worry may have made them make mistakes but in the end they all put justice above all else.

Ron started to say something but his words were drowned out by Lenny's loud baritone voice. "Okay, let's cut to the chase, shall we? What happened?" Lenny demanded, "What exactly happened to Kat and Jimmy? Who set them up to be trapped in that tunnel at Mare Vista? Was it James?"

Angel piped in, obviously still not trusting him, "He took the call when Jimmy called Kat and said he thought he knew where the missing pages are hidden... in tunnel leading from house barn.... LJ was the one that led Kat into the tunnel, but it was a setup! Someone set them up? Who if not James, knew where they were going?"

"Maybe Sal overheard and tipped off the bad guys." Antoinette murmured. "Or maybe Linda Amoretti overheard! Yes, that must've been it. She heard and made a call to her dad, Johnny Amoretti. He's a hitman, right?" Antoinette breathlessly cried out.

"Yes, but… " Cassandra stammered. "But I can't get Jimmy's words to her out of my mind. Remember he said, 'I'm sorry Kat. I had to do this.' He knew they walked into a trap!"

"Yes!" Caroline said with a sob in her voice, "They were cornered at both ends by rats! Thankfully Ron, and Jack got there in time!"

Angel jumped to her feet and dramatically swooned, "They saved Kat and Jimmy in the nick of time! They covered both ends or the tunnel; thereby catching the rats in their own trap! Meanwhile, Little Jimmy pulled Kat into a side culvert/drain, that takes them next to the old winery and barn, where they climbed the fence and crawled into her Jeep to wait for their heroes." Angel's romantic description brought laughter which ended what was becoming a tense moment in the library.

But the comic relief was short-lived. "No! I know Ron, Lenny, and Jack had a few close calls on the mountain. And Lenny took a bloody fall on at least one occasion," Antoinette said suspiciously remembering Lenny falling into a freshly dug pit coming home banged up and bloody. "I thought it was Jimmy setting you up, until last night. But could it have been Jack? It had to be Jack! The close calls and traps were... never when Jack was out of the loop,"

"Yeah", Ron said dryly looking Jack in the eye. "I've been suspicious of you for a long time, Jack. It wasn't very long ago that you were a sloppy out of shape punk repo man; now you're fit, dressing like a million bucks—and driving a $40,000 vehicle and engaged to a beautiful woman. So, what's the score, Jack? Are you a red herring or a snake in the grass?" The room was silenced. The Insiders were shocked, until both Ron and Jack burst out laughing.

"For crying out loud people! I've worked with this guy for ten years. I know him. I trust him. He has money because Bill Norris, who trusts him impeccably, gives him referrals when he hears of someone in search of a super-sleuth, since my wife is never available!" This brought the house down and any further suspicion off Jack.

"I think we all need a little break," Catarina stood up, this time her smile was strained. "Eduardo and Sal will go to the kitchen and see what they can stir up; in the meantime, this is a perfect time to stroll the grounds or even hike to the top of the hill for a bird's eye view of the inn," her throat caught and she had to clear it while reaching for a hankie from her pocket.

"And of Konocti reflected onto Clear Lake," Kat added hoping to take the attention off Catarina's near emotional break. "The mid-morning hike is almost as good as the sunrise..." Kat stopped mid-sentence remembering it was why she got the call here in the first place. And then wondered how Jimmy knew to reach her here. Looking back at Cassandra, she knew she was wondering the same thing. Walking over to sit near her best friend, Kat whispered, "That little stinker! He must've put a tracking device on my Jeep, too!"

The thought of stretching their legs with a morning stroll appealed to the Insiders. They also wanted to digest all the things and events discussed, not just this morning but the prior evening as well. They had seen the gazebo and pool as they drove up the driveway the evening of the Celebration of Life-turned-Reveal Celebration, as well as from the library; and all of their rooms had lakeview windows, decks or balconies. But that's not the same as walking the grounds, smelling the fresh air, and feeling a light breeze on your face. They found the paths that wound around the grounds to be even more lovely than they imagined; with statuary and water features and the fragrance of the multiple varieties of plants and flowers.

As she watched Cassandra walk in that direction hand in hand with Jack, Kat was reminded of the many courtship walks and hikes with Ron. It was a very long time since she had any thoughts of romance. As her eyes met with Ron's, she knew he was having similar thoughts. They smiled and both made a mental note for their next date to be a night at the inn. With all that had been happening, they had not had any time alone for several months. In fact, last night was the first time in over two months that they were alone in the house—just the three of them. And although they loved all the time they've had

89

with Baby Ronnie, they felt the need for a date—not so much a date night; a morning sunrise walk, too, with a thermos of coffee to drink on the top of the hill seated on the wonderful cement benches leaning on the cement table with vines carved into the bases of both table and benches. Kat sighed at the thought.

Although she and Ron were yearning to take the hike to the top of the hill overlooking the great house that looked out over the lake to Konocti, this morning they knew it would have to wait until date night. Because right now, Mrs. Capra would need assistance to make it to the gazebo just below the house.

All the guests had heard stories of the beautiful B&B perched on the hillside with panoramic views and some had been there before. However, this was the first visit for some; regardless, all were excited to walk as much of the grounds as they could. Some made it to the top and some only part way before turning back to join others who had picked a spot to soak up the sunshine and views.

Angel, who had joined one of Catarina's groups, played tour guide to those planning on making the trek to the top, starting the tour as they stepped off the veranda: "You'll notice off to the left of the pool is a large sauna, and beyond that is a path through lush greenery and Johnny-jump-ups that led past statues, benches, and fountains; and finally to the large gazebo."

As they reached the gazebo, Angel said, nonchalantly, but looking directly at Cassandra, "This has been the setting for many weddings," then in a hushed voice, as if she was seeing Cassandra and Jack exchanging vows there, "in fact, I overheard

90

Catarina saying they have one scheduled next month."

Angel glanced at Lydia, who had already started panting and cocked her head to the nearby bench, and winked. The grateful Lydia sat down next to Mrs. Capra, as James was serving lemon water to those in and around the gazebo.

The path continued down around the lawn, to some steps where a mermaid fountain beckoned from the center of a cement pond, which it filled, causing water to spill, forming a waterfall that flowed and bubbled along next to the path; before running under a footbridge. "Yes!" Theo said under her breath, "Just as I remember it from the first time." Though the group hurried along behind Angel, Theo just stood there dazed and frozen as if her feet were planted along with the lush shrubs and flowers. She was missing her group and was saddened that this month's session had been canceled. Now she knew why.

Theo noticed that other hikers had stopped to enjoy the view.

Angel's voice calling her name as well as others brought her back to reality. "Another favorite photo spot for brides," Angel was saying, over her shoulder, as she crossed over the footbridge leading the group onward and upward.

Something about the lush greenery and path, passing a mermaid and fish, brought memories of childhood games for some. For Theo, it brought memories of her first walk with the group made up of strangers who she now meets back here at the inn once a month; some who, along with Catarina, turned out to be her sisters and are all her family. This

91

brought the painful thought that much of the trauma that Kat and Jimmy had gone through was brought on by her ex-husband and his gangster associates. She recalled how the spa membership she and five other women won seven years prior had turned into a nightmare by those very gangsters! Theo shuddered and shook off the memory before it could spoil her hike. She quickly caught up with the rest of the group and laughed at cute and bubbly Angel springing up the path expecting everyone to keep up. She also noticed that John Buchanan had no trouble staying a respectable distance behind Angel.

Soon the path came to stairs followed by another path and then more stairs; and then more. Before they knew it, the group realized they were climbing the hill. Angel relentlessly led them up the stairs that followed yet another waterfall and followed it to its beginning. The group stopped— partly because they were mesmerized by the water bubbling up from a natural spring in the rocks, but mostly to catch their breaths.

Angel didn't run out of stories and tidbits about the history, rumors, and legends surrounding the old house and its former owners, ones that Dominic had told the group she met with. Her love for the place was apparent; and Theo couldn't help but wonder if perhaps it wasn't Cassandra and Jack that she had thought of back at the gazebo. That is before she saw a certain look pass between Angel and John Buchanan.

The tour continued up the path that went further than the women had expected. It turned into quite a hike. Angel walked slower now, as the trail was so pretty with its different exotic plants and trees. She took the time to point out and name each one along the way, giving both the common name and scientific one; neither of which the group would remember, but all of which they enjoyed hearing.

Among the huffing and puffing Theo had a flashback of a shadowy figure appearing and then disappearing in the thick wooded areas only to appear again at another bend, following them as they made the trek up the mountainside. Again, she had to push the negative memories out and as she breathed in the fresh mountain air, she replaced those thoughts with one of affirmations that Catarina had drilled into her group's minds. Let go of the past to embrace the present and look to the future.

As Theo once again mentally joined the hikers, she focused on Angel who was saying, "It's rumored that the original owner of the house was an arborist who collected plants and trees from all over the world, and whose goal was to create an arboretum." Theo recognized this speech as the one Dominic told her women's group so many years ago. "Which is why you may be surprised by many of the plants and trees you'll see here at Crossroads. Few are native to Lake County," Angel continued while pointing to a grove of olive trees up ahead, which caused Cassandra to chuckle.

The group stopped and looked at Cassandra, wanting to be let in on the joke. Embarrassed, she murmured, "It's nothing…just that Kat and I had nailed a couple boards to a couple of olive trees once and called it a love seat. We daydreamed about the man we would one day marry." This put smiles on everyone's faces, none smiled more than Jack. Angel grinned and turned to point out one tree in particular that she had always loved and planned on drawing it one day at the art classes held at Crossroads. The big gnarly old tree had an old tattered tire swing dangling from one of the tired old branches. Once again, Theo was drawn to a memory of her group and stood gazing at the swing as if in a trance until one of the hikers tugged at her arm to get her moving again. Reluctantly she picked up the pace to rejoin the group; but would remember the olive tree swing again that night just before falling asleep, and smile as she thought of her little sister Maddie, and her older brother, James.

To the group's relief, Angel finally slowed down and led them to a grouping of benches where there were plenty of plants and statues for her to talk about as an excuse to stop a little longer than necessary. When it seemed apparent that all of her charges had rested enough, she was on the move again. But not as fast. All in all, it was a very pleasant hike for the Insiders. The hikers thoroughly enjoyed the history of the estate; as well as admired Angel's enthusiasm. Someone mentioned it and another laughed and said, "It comes with youth!" Lenny grunted, "Or leaves with youth!" which made everyone laugh, causing some of Lenny's anger to leave.

Just when the Insiders thought for sure they had hiked to the ocean, the trail took a turn, giving a glimpse of the house far below, and a panoramic view of the lake and mountain that was beyond breathtaking! The impressive views of Clear Lake and Mount Konocti from the guests' suites paled in comparison with this view! "Definitely worth the hike up the hill again!" Theo panted and had a sense of déjà-vu, until she recalled that she had said almost those exact words her first time seeing this view.

A wonderful cement table was perched near the edge of a flat colorful sandstone-paved terrace carved out of the hillside. Tiny native grasses mixed with clover and chamomile grew in between the pavers. The cement table appeared to be stone as well, with a carved grapevine motif twining up the legs; cement seats surrounded it which had been molded to look like tree stumps, again with the grapevine motif twining around them. On the table someone, most likely James and Sal, had hiked up the back way and left paper cups and a large jar of iced lemon water and trays of finger sandwiches for the Insiders.

Angel invited the group to sit and after brief conversation, there was silence as they all sat quietly eating and drinking up the lemon water—as well as the view. A regatta was sailing under Konocti and once again Theo considered moving to this wonderful county of Lake.

"I could get used to this life!" Cassandra said bringing a wishful smile to everyone's lips.

After a few minutes, Angel said, "Well, I suppose they will be gathering in the library soon," and started picking up the cups and stashing them in a bag which she pulled out of her backpack, letting the group know it was time to resume their trek. How thankful they were that the path now took a turn down the hill. The rooftop of Crossroads Inn Time far below disappeared as they turned a bend, only to reappear at the next bend with a closer view of its tower and a *widow's walk* that they had not noticed earlier. For the first time, they saw that Crossroads

Inn Time was strategically located on a point which jutted out, giving the inn the benefit of lake views from three sides. The back of the house was built into the hillside causing the otherwise stately house to look a bit lopsided. There was something else some of them hadn't seen before, but some were staying in one of the neat row of cottages and tiny cabins behind the garage and what looked like an ornate greenhouse.

The path was a little steep and the women hadn't planned on a hike; after all, they had dressed for a memorial so the descent was slow and careful. Theo chuckled to herself as she remembered her dear friend Rita calling out "Miss Molly Good Golly! If I start to fall, run for your lives! I'll roll over ya'll like a steam roller." Then she had broken into the blues song, ♪ "I'm a Steamroller Bay-bah! And I'm a gonna Roll all ovah you!"

As the Insiders walked, conversation returned to the mystery they had all been drawn into trying solve and Lenny loudly repeated his earlier question: "So who set them up? Who set my niece and Jimmy up?" He was obviously mad at Jimmy because he had not referred to him as Little Jimmy or even the shortened LJ since the night before. "So anyways, I guess we've ruled out Sal? But I had my money on him. Wasn't it Salvatore who was coerced or conned into thinking he was only securing a position for himself, and joined the bad guys?"

Angel replied, "Yeah, I thought so too," but then she reminded everyone, "Realization set in that he was not only conned but disloyal to 'his family', and turned state's witness. And at great risk to himself continued working 'undercover' for Ron.

96

Pretending to be Johnny's flunky couldn't have been easy either, from what I saw of the jerk. Brave man, that Sal." She said this for her friend Tessie's benefit even though she wasn't present.

"What about Jimmy?" Cassandra repeated what she had said to Kat earlier, "I mean all that was happening, do you think he was going to throw Kat under the bus, so to speak, but saw the escape tunnel? I mean those words *'I'm sorry Kat. I had to go along with this.'* I can't stop thinking about those words."

"Since Jimmy and his dad were working with the Feds they must've known the inn's phones were tapped," Angel defended LJ, "and Ron most likely told Sal, but not even *he* knew which perp was behind calling in a hit on Kat and Jimmy.

"But the point is that when Jimmy knew things were closing in on him, he called Kat. He would've known that not only Linda would listen in, but the Feds would also be listening. Jimmy also knew Kat sometimes met with her group for a sunrise walk, so he called Kat at Crossroads, knowing Linda would be listening, and told her to pick him up because he had found out something was hidden in the tunnel at Mare Vista. When Kat resisted, he said if she didn't come and get him right now, he would find another way there, even if he had to ride his bike and catch a bus. He knew the protective 'Mom' Kat would ditch the group to pick him up. Jimmy probably called her a few more times, so by now the Feds would be following the pings on her cell phone. And would have a tail on them. By the time they were on Silverado Trail, the Feds would know where they were heading and could pass them without being noticed and be all set up with a trap."

"Yeah, but no." Lenny cut in, "You both watch too much TV. How would they know it was in the tunnel and how would they know to let the bad guys go first? It had to be a total setup! Jimmy knew he and Kat would be caught in a trap set by rats. But, he also knew someone was setting a better trap to catch the rats. Before Jimmy called Kat, Ron, Jack and I were lured to separate locations. I was sent to a place we'd been investigating up on Cobb, and they got sent to a clearing on Mount Umunhum, that is just above Mare Vista. Both locations were wild goose chases; but it put Ron and Jack in position to catch the rats. Someone orchestrated it! *And cut me out!* I want to know who and why!" Then muttering mostly to himself, he back-tracked the incident, "As Kat & Jimmy were entering the tunnel, Ron caught a call that sent him and Jack running to each end of tunnel, to save Kat and Jimmy. My cell phone was jammed so I was still on Cobb waiting for Ron's call." Lenny growled, "I didn't get a call until after all was said and done. The bad guys were in cuffs; and Jimmy, Kat, and Ron were secretly heading back to Lake County in her Jeep. Ron said they took a roundabout way home so as not to be seen. Yeah! *Not seen by me!*," growled Lenny again. "I was deliberately kept out of the loop and I am going to find out why!"

Angel changed the subject. "Jimmy said he knew there was a drainage from the Mare Vista tunnel, he may have already been there."

"No doubt!" her Uncle Lenny said sarcastically.

"Anyway, he knew he and Kat were small enough to crawl in. He knew it would be tight, but he didn't expect to have flashbacks of Konocti Caves, and Kat comforted him and talked him through it, which would have remained their secret if LJ himself didn't bring it up."

"Back on track!" Lenny ordered his niece, seeing she was displaying sympathy to someone he thought a person of interest. "Ok, so they escaped while Ron and Jack trapped the hitmen Guido and Enzo. After the perps were caught in said trap, the head perp, whoever that may be—Annunzio the head of the Los Gatos Mob family maybe... "

"Or Steven Pinero, my good-for-nothing rat of an ex-husband!" blurted Theo.

"LJ said it wasn't Johnny or I'd put my money on him," said Lenny, then realized he was taking the word of someone he earlier considered a suspect.

Angel took advantage of his pause and got back on her theory: "Guido? or perhaps Francesca? Or both? Anyway, someone received a text saying pests were caught in the trap and taken care of. And that they would return to their fishing boats and lay low for a while. But they had actually been arrested. Either Ron or Bill Norris sent the text using Guido's cell phone."

Lenny interjected, "Leaving Kat... and Jimmy to safely go into hiding at Kat and Ron's Edgewater home, where they put together all the rest of the puzzles and solved more than one mystery and planned one heck of a Fumaroles Reveal Party!" He chuckled in spite of himself.

Much to Angel's relief, her Uncle Lenny finally seemed to have made peace with being out of the loop, and she heaved a heavy sigh, causing Lenny to give her a look. She pretended to be getting winded and said, "I'm so tired!" "Doubtful," is all Lenny said.

Then John Buchanan, who had been unusually quiet, suddenly spoke up, "But who set up the perps? Little Jimmy?"

"Not by himself," Lenny growled. "It would've been the same person that tipped Ron that Kat was stepping into a trap."

Jack replied, speaking out for the first time. "And it couldn't have been LJ, because he was with Kat."

Angel agreed, "That's right!" And added, "That was pretty tricky. He couldn't be told too soon, because Ron would never have let Kat be used for bait."

"That I already knew," Lenny snarled. "But still, someone was playing their cards close to the vest because if he wasn't told soon enough, the bad guys could've... "

"So, who were all the bad guys, and who was the leader? I mean someone must've been calling the shots. Pulling the strings, like LJ said last night in the game. WHO WAS IT?" Angel yelled, having come to the end of her patience.

"Well, that we still don't know, but my money is still on Jimmy," Lenny snarled again. "Anyways, he's involved somehow. At Kat's expense!" Clearly still mad at Jimmy.

The path led the group to a long steep staircase carved from the natural stone terrain; and the female Insiders with uncomfortable shoes were grateful for the pipe railing to cling to. The stairway eventually descended down next to the stone bleachers of the amphitheater.

"They've had some fine plays here put on by local theater groups," Angel tried to change the subject, seeing things were getting too emotional and regretted bringing it up again.

"And games," John tried to joke about the previous night's event, then quickly regretted it when Angel shot him a look! "Too soon?" he grimaced, and she rolled her eyes and continued, "Occasionally, we have some midweek shows, perhaps we'll have one while we are here," she smiled at Cassandra whose heart skipped a beat. Cassandra knew she loved the theater. Nothing could help her forget herself, or her life, faster or more thoroughly than a play. She had season tickets to the local Soper Reese Theater and went to as many school plays as she had time for. "I think I must've been to something here, she pondered."

"It's possible," Angel smiled, she was back in tour guide mode: "This inn has been here quite a long time, and has had several lives. It was even a foster child retreat for a while, I understand." Theo looked up from the plant she had bent over to look at closer.

Angel made one more stop before leading the Insiders back to the house.

"The inn starts their vegetables here in this greenhouse; and transplants them after threat of frost has passed. But James also has several flowers, shrubs and trees going on in here at all times too. Some are rare and pretty exotic." By the time Angel finished giving her dissertation on the many plants in the greenhouse, the Insiders were well past ready to

101

return to the library, but first make a stop at the powder room and gentleman's room off the veranda, the very ones elegant partiers freshened up in the previous evening. To the Insiders, last night's event now seemed a lifetime ago.

Angel, followed by the tired but exhilarated Insiders, entered the house through French doors off the large back veranda. Then they made their triumphant entrance into the library where the others were waiting; looking like canaries who caught the cat. Seems like both groups had resolved some of their issues. But it still remained to be determined who set up the perps!

"What's for lunch?" asked John Buchanan, as a mouthwatering aroma drifted from the kitchen.

"What? We just watched you single-handedly clear a platter of sandwiches," Jack laughed, and everyone joined in. After they stopped laughing at John's incredible appetite, Catarina timidly said she had a question, knowing how Kat felt about the person she was about to call into question.

Kat was quiet but Ron said "Yes, Catarina? What is it?"

"Well… Mrs. Capra..."

"What about Mrs. Capra?" Kat demanded too quickly.

"Well, how does she fit in?" Then seeing Kat getting riled up again, she rephrased it, "I mean *does* she fit in here somehow? I've thought for years she was hiding something. Does she have a past? Since she's still here, I guess she's not a suspect in this case.

But where's her husband? She never speaks of him. Maybe her husband had something to do with all this?"

Ron started to say something, but Mrs. Capra put her hand up as if to stop him, and said, "No, Ron. I'll tell her. I need to tell this. I need to *finally tell this*." She began by relating a romance that she once hinted at long ago watching her foster boys with Angel and John Buchanan up at the Lombardi Foster Home. After a moment and wiping a tear, Mrs. Capra continued, "My husband was in the Service when I met him. I worked at the base commissary. We were attracted to each other right away, even though he was much older than me, in fact he was about to retire after twenty years of service, but got orders for Vietnam. He insisted we get married before he left. He said he wanted to make sure I was taken care of if anything… well if…" Wiping her eyes again, the frail elderly widow continued. "We both had wanted children. Me more than him, probably. But it wasn't to be. He was in country—I believe that's the term. Anyway, he wasn't there long when…" Mrs. Capra paused, choosing her words. "He was over there just a short time when he… well…" stopping to choose her words, she backtracked.

"He had been caught up in a terrifying battle, and was wounded and got lost from his company. He wandered for days in the jungle hurting and bleeding, and finally found his way to a village. He realized he had somehow walked across the border. He made a quick and regrettable decision to…" Mrs. Capra swallowed hard and blurted, "Instead of attaching himself to the nearest platoon, he chose to go AWOL." The old woman hung her head in shame.

103

"Sometime later he came home on a junket. By then I had received the insurance money, bought the house, and since I had no desire to marry again, I decided to be a mother to many and started my foster home. After a few months in my home, I started getting the feeling that someone else was there when it was only me. It was him. My husband hid in the attic to keep his eye on me. He loved me, but was ashamed. *So ashamed.* He didn't want me to know he was a deserter. I knew he was up there. I was just happy he was alive and near me. That's all I cared about. Just that he was safe. And he was home. I didn't want him captured and sent to the brig. So, I just pretended I didn't know..." Mrs. Capra's voice drifted off, and she sat toying with the man's initialed hanky in her hands, which she always kept in her pocket, wrapped around the locket which held the photo of the man she'd always loved.

After a few moments of silence, Mrs. Capra began speaking again, relieved she could finally tell the story. "Early one morning, I unexpectedly came upon him in the garden picking a couple of tomatoes. He looked like a cornered rabbit. I pretended not to recognize him and to not know he'd been staying in the attic. I offered him a job as gardener and handyman. He accepted, but I've always thought he knew full well I recognized him. But what mattered at the time was now we could at least sit in the garden and have iced tea, or coffee and sandwiches or soup sometimes. We could at last talk to each other, if only about the garden, the house repairs, the weather... but, never mentioning he slept in the attic, never acknowledging our work talk a Real but talk love Angel gently asked.

"Well, one night I did go to the attic to confront him. But he looked so scared. Like a deer in the headlights! When I saw the pleading look in his eyes, I backed down. So, I just told him that I wanted him to know that I knew he was living in my attic and it was okay with me. To live there… *with me*.

"I said it was okay as long as he behaved, he could have a safe, dry place to be... but he must *never* let my boys know he lived in the attic. And then I just continued to act like I didn't know he was my husband, and from then on, by night…" Mrs. Capra grew quiet and stared blankly at the window.

Kat, who knew the story, continued for Mrs. Capra, "Mr. Capra hid in Mrs. Capra's attic by night, and by day, he hid in plain sight, as her gardener and handyman, all those years, keeping his eye on her, until his recent death. Learning about his death is what brought on her stroke. The hospital called when he had been brought in and the only identification he had was her name and address in his pocket. True love," Kat said, dabbing at her own eyes.

"My own true love," Mrs. Capra's voice cracked and she became quiet, refusing to even try to speak again.

Kat answered the few questions asked, before restating, "Mrs. Capra got the news of his death, which led to her heart attack and stroke."

Someone in the back of the room whispered "True love," again, and the room went silent.

After an appropriate moment of silence, John Buchanan asked gently, "Was he related to anyone connected to all this? I guess I should say, since everyone seems to be connected somehow to Little

105

Jimmy, how was Mr. Capra connected?"

Mrs. Capra sighed as if it was the question she had dreaded and nodded before answering, "One day while he was working in the garden, I went up to the attic to clean and was gathering his laundry when I found his journal... I felt guilty reading it, but I had to know how bad it was... I mean, I knew it must've been terrible for him to do what he did."

Mrs. Capra suddenly turned into the grizzly bear Ron grew to know and love. She looked squarely at each face in the room before saying, "I'll have no one judging him. *Not a soul!* And this is to never be repeated. Not *ever!*" Mrs. Capra waited to continue her story until everyone, including Kat and Ron, had nodded a promise of secrecy. "Yes, my husband had a connection to Little Jimmy, but it was a roundabout way. His connection was to Crossroads, and James and Catarina." Glancing at them both, Mrs. Capra continued, "Although he was much older than your father, they served in the army together."

Looking at Theo, she said softly, "Your father had joined the platoon almost the same time as my husband... fresh out of boot camp, he was. And greener than anyone Sarge had ever seen. Sarge... that's what everyone called my husband. He was a First Sergeant," Mrs. Capra added proudly. "The Kid—that's what Sarge called your father in his journal, or sometimes Lewy The Kid, because of his last name—The Kid quickly turned to drink and whatever else he could get his hands on to numb his fear. While in the bush one night, The Kid rambled on about his wife's inheritance. And how if he made it back, he'd be a rich man someday. He'd gone on and on about the documents in a suitcase in the attic, and how he'd come across them, unbeknownst to her, when they were dating." Looking up at Theo again she said, "Your grandmother had sent him to the attic to find holiday decorations, and he opened the wrong suitcase. He didn't let on that he'd found the Trust papers. He didn't want anyone thinking he was only interested in her inheritance. He truly loved the girl, your mother. Anyway, the more he drank the more he talked, and as he spoke, he became enraged that the Army was keeping him from his new bride. The next day, he was gone. Before Sarge got up enough courage to come find me, he wandered the streets of San Francisco, hanging out in bars with vets, and ran into The Kid there. It was inevitable that they would run into each other. Lewy The Kid didn't know my husband had deserted, but one night after drinking most of a bottle of cheap gin, Sarge told him." Once again, her eyes filled with tears spilling down her face. Her hand was trembling as she tried to pull her hankie out to catch her tears. "My husband was filled with guilt when The Kid told him how his wife had thought he'd died, until he showed up at her door. He realized the pain I must be feeling, and resolved to find me.

"The Kid said he didn't stay with his wife long before he left her, because she objected to his drinking. He talked The Kid into going back home to his wife, which he did… but after a while he returned to the streets. He couldn't leave Nam behind. Or the drinking. And his wife hated how both had changed him. But The Kid had changed. He was hateful and mean-spirited. It was more than the war or drinking. He said he discovered that his wife had cheated on him while he was fighting the war. And he told Sarge

107

how he *fixed her wagon* for good. He said he took her future along with her dirty past, the suitcase in the attic, which now also held baby clothes and adoption papers. He said he buried it all where she would never find it. It would be right under her feet, but she'd never know. 'Just like she tried to hide her cheating under my nose' he told my husband. I wasn't sure until I learned James' real name is James Dominic Lewis a while back when all that was going on with Theo's husband and the Mob. Lewy The Kid's last name was Lewis. And when I heard the story about how James being with his father when he buried a suitcase full of documents and baby clothes in the yard of Crossroads, well… So, yes, I knew about the Trust… the buried treasure as it were—*after the fact*. And since I didn't have any useful information… And I didn't know…" Mrs. Capra stopped and exchanged glances with Kat. "I never knew how Little Jimmy was related." Shaking her head and tears falling again. This time she didn't try to catch them. "I never knew…"

Again Mrs. Capra stopped short as Catarina shot her a glance.

Then looking directly at Lydia, Catarina said coldly, "Lydia, James' drunken father told your husband, Cabbie, who then told you the story the drunk told him while driving him to and from Lake County." Lydia just stared back at Catarina. "The documents… did you know what the documents were? That they were concerning Crossroads Inn and Mount Hannah that had been with the birth and adoption papers, and clothing that fell out of the suitcase that the drunken father threw into the hole he dug."

108

Kat couldn't remain quiet either. She had to say what she was wondering. "Had you been blackmailing the father, and is that how you really have so much money?"

The tears and wailing that came out of the stout old woman had Kat and Catarina on their feet in no time consoling and trying to calm her. "How could we say such things? How could we *even think* such a thing about you?" Kat said.

Catarina added, "You have the biggest, purest heart of anyone I've ever known. I'm sorry. So, so sorry! Please forgive me. Please forgive us!"

Kat was consumed with guilt. Catarina had told her the story of how James and her drunken father was picked up by Cabbie, Lydia's husband, and hired Cabbie to drive him to and from Lake County. She described how the drunk raved all the way there, where he planned on picking up some kids. But only a young boy and an infant were picked up for the return trip back to San Francisco where the infant was dropped off, before the boy—before *James*—was left at a rundown home in a ghetto. The infant was Catarina.

Kat had suspected Lydia of withholding information about the ongoing case. That's why she told Ron to invite her to the Memorial. She was *so wrong!* Lydia was not involved in this case at all. She was just a Red Herring.

"But wait a minute!" John Buchanan shouted. Then in a calm, deliberate voice he said, "Let me get this straight. James heard the story, too?" Looking at James, he directed his questions to him, "You heard your father's ranting? You saw him bury the suitcase? You knew about the documents? Did you contrive the entire story about being related to all those women just to get your hands on the treasure buried on Crossroads Inn grounds? James, when you got out of the Vet Hospital and were wandering the streets in San Francisco going to one Vet bar to the next, did you run into Jimmy's dad? Did you recognize him when he started showing up doing odd jobs around the county? Did the two of you concoct this whole story of being Jimmy's dad just to get your hands on the entire fortune—not just Crossroads? But the whole shebang!"

Ron groaned and thought, "This kid *really doesn't know anything* about how this works—son of a high sheriff or not." Out loud he said, "Whoa there, John! Pull back your reins. First of all, the fact that he was at Crossroads *with his mother* at the time of the parental kidnapping, and he rode in the cab back to San Francisco with his dad, makes him brother to all his mother's children which would be Catarina, Theo, and Maddie. And secondly, of course James knew about the documents. That's what the whole thing was about back in 2012, when they all won that cockamamie spa membership that Catarina cooked up to get him and his sisters all together, hoping Maddie would remember what she saw that night, so they could find the buried documents."

"Okay." John said meekly and sat down.

"While we're on the subject of James," Antoinette said, "I have a question for him. How did you find one journal in the wall, but missed the other journal and documents that Sal found? I can't help wondering if you two conspired together to try selling it. Did you?"

"*No!*" James and Sal said simultaneously.

"Sal found the other stuff while I was off delivering Carolina Jane's second journal to Catarina and Eduardo. It took me so long, because... well... I stopped to read her last entry. I just wanted to know if she recovered from her amnesia, but I found out about her ties to Crossroads. And I kept quiet about it for a while. To think it out. I never told anyone until I told Catarina, and she and Eduardo convinced me to turn the missing pages over to Ron. Which I did, but I cut the pages out and hid them... I *never even thought* of selling the journal to our foes. It was just that, when I realized Catarina and Eduardo... *my family* would lose Crossroads..."

Catarina jumped in, "But *he did* finally come forth with them."

Smiling gratefully at his sister, trying hard to hide his sadness, James said, "So Ron, looks like you are the legal heir to Crossroads. Congratulations then." James said, trying to show no emotion.

Ron looked confused, but replied, "Yes, I am... but... didn't Catarina and Eduardo tell you? I *abdicated*... Kat and I discussed it last night and she totally agreed with me. There is no way that I am desirous of taking a business that someone else put their heart into. You all are, as Kat put it, 'attached by the heart to each other and to Crossroads Inn Time Bed & Breakfast and Spa.' Besides you're all Kat's family. That means *you're mine*, too." Ron grinned, seeing the relief wash over James, while everyone in the room clapped and cheered. Almost everyone.

John Buchanan's face had almost stopped blushing in embarrassment, when he heard Antoinette say his name. "Oh, no! Now what?" he groaned silently and tried to scrunch his tall body deeper into his chair.

Antoinette's question about him caused a few eyebrows to raise, "Last night, Little Jimmy suggested that your father sent you to spy on Ron and earlier to infiltrate the Retreat on Cobb Mountain to get next to Heather Logan. Weren't your fingerprints found on a water bottle near her body? And isn't the retreat where you first became acquainted with my niece, the *much younger* Angel Amoretti? And didn't you try using that relationship to infiltrate Ron's family at the request of your father?"

"Auntie!" cried a mortified Angel. Antoinette had just disclosed to, you may as well say, the whole county, that Angel had been in treatment. Not only that, but she insinuated that she and John were an item! Angel couldn't take any more humiliation and she ran out of the library.

Her brother-in-law stood up to rescue Angel's good name. "Yes, Angel has offered her *volunteer service* at several places around the county. One area in which she volunteered was helping troubled or sick children with horse therapy—which is her career choice and for which she is getting her degree. As for John—yes, they *may* have met at the retreat. John and Angel are both *very generous* with their time and volunteer at quite a few organizations. And sometimes they happen to volunteer at the same time."

Ron looked squarely at his wife's aunt, "Antoinette, you've been asking most of the questions tonight, and I actually have a couple of questions for *you*! But I'm saving them for when we have more time. Lots more *time*." Ron said putting a strong emphasis on time. He was not doing a good job of holding back his temper. He paused a moment and locked eyes with Kat, who seemed shocked to hear him speak to her Auntie that way. Ron regained control, but he made a mental note that his comment obviously hit a raw nerve with Antoinette.

"And let me just also say this about John," having seen what it looks like from the audience's point of view. Ron was now clearly trying to make up for being so brutal before with John, "From childhood John's father has used and manipulated him. The former high sheriff and congressional candidate would do *anything* to advance his career. He even stooped so low as to use his wife's suicide to get sympathy votes. But to John's credit, he started seeing through his father and stopped being a willing patsy for him. John is a really good guy. A stand-up guy! And when he started seeing through his dad and…"

John stood up again, "Thanks Ron, I appreciate your kind words. But I'd like to speak for myself on this matter and address the issues raised about me."

As Ron sat down, he avoided eye contact with Kat. He wondered if what just happened was going to come between his wife and himself. Kat was protective about her family, and until now there had never been an issue with them. He felt bad about losing his self-control.

Kat studied her husband's profile and body language. She couldn't help seeing that Ron had come down on Antoinette so hard in retaliation for how she cruelly humiliated Angel. He was sticking up for her little sister. Kat was at the same time proud *and disturbed.* Although she was angry as Ron was that her aunt had outed Angel and John's rehab, she wondered if Ron's behavior was *just* about that. She suspected there was something else. Kat had learned a bit herself, from listening to Ron's sessions with Dr. Fleming and up until now she hadn't suspected her husband of holding anything back about the case. Now she wondered if Ron had uncovered something about Auntie Antoinette. Something sinister. "No! Auntie? Impossible! I don't believe it!" Kat muttered. Ron involuntarily turned his head to look at her. Their eyes locked. Kat no longer wondered. Kat was now certain; her husband knew something about her aunt that he wasn't sharing with her.

Ron and Kat both turned their attention to John and tried to focus on what he was sharing. "The older I got, and yes, the more therapy I received, the more I could remember about… about my mother's *so-called* suicide. And the more I remembered, the more I had to follow my gut feelings about my dad. First of all, yes, my mother was depressed. Her unhappy life with a self-absorbed, demanding, never satisfied and unappreciative, narcissistic husband would make anyone depressed. And I can attest to the mental, emotional, and yes sometimes physical abuse she endured. But I know… I am *certain* she would *never* have committed suicide in the grotesque way…" John had to stop and compose himself. "She knew I would be walking through that door all alone. She would never have done that to me. My father, on the other hand... well, like Ron said my father would do anything to further his self-interests. *Anything*! I already knew about my father's crooked campaign promises. I also think he jumped at the opportunity to villainize my mother in the public's and my eyes

114

so he could use me to soak up sympathy *and* votes." Lowering his voice, John added, "That was the year he was elected sheriff." Then clearing his voice, John stood taller and sounded stronger. "Realizing all this was why I had started visiting the Simmons' household. I was looking for an opportunity to bring up my suspicions to Ron. And as for Angel... yes, your being there *was a bonus*." John said to Angel who had returned and was standing in the doorway. Then to Antoinette he said, "And yes, she is younger than me. But not that much… and she *is so much* more mature than me." Looking back at Angel he said, "I was attracted to your strength. Not your vulnerability. I never saw you as vulnerable. I saw your passion and how you pour your heart into everything you do. I know I am weak. Sure, my appearance belies that fact, and it has gotten me through life—for a while. But inside, I'm still that scared little kid standing at a closed door afraid of what's on the other side. But Angel, this is a door I want to open. I understand I must wait until you are ready to unlock it. I'll wait. Now that my dad is completely off my back, I can choose my own path. To be honest I let my dad push me in any direction he chose. I didn't have a *clue* which path to take. Which direction to go... or what to be. But when I saw how you brought those kids out of the dark place they were hiding, well I was helped too. And I feel strongly that horse therapy is a much-needed service. It can help autistic kids and adults alike in our community. And I want to help you make that happen." Winking at Jack, John said, "Now that a super sleuth P.I. uncovered the trust my mother left me, and recommended an out-of-county attorney

115

who is working on getting it released to me, I will have that to utilize towards that goal. The goal of making horse therapy readily available in Lake County. Believe me when I tell you, this in no way has anything to do with my personal feelings for you. I'm offering my help and funding with no strings attached." But by the look in Angel's eyes, Kat suspected strings soon might not be so unwelcome. She hoped she was right. She wanted her little sister to find happiness and true love like she did. And Ron was right. John Buchanan *is* a stand-up guy.

Catarina stood up, breaking the silence, she announced dinner would be served on the veranda shortly and suggested the guests might wish to return to their rooms to freshen up. She also informed them that she had taken the liberty to provide them all with new sweat pants, tank tops and hoodies. "A trick I learned from Lydia," she said, and gave Lydia a sweet smile which Lydia tried to return.

It had been a long and emotionally trying day for everyone. Dinner was quiet and there was no after dinner visiting. No one seemed in the mood for conversation, or games.

However, after Dr. Fleming stood, looked at his watch and nonchalantly told the Insiders he had a group meeting on the mountain, and bid them goodbye until breakfast, and he took his leave, Antoinette stood up and facing the Insiders she demanded, *"What about Dr Fleming?"* Pausing to get everyone's attention before continuing, "I remember how poor terrified Kat was chased and she drove to the retreat thinking it would be safe. Only to find an ice-cold doctor who barely spoke to her. Her mother and I were there when you brought her home. I've never seen her so scared and upset. She was a mess!" Kat shot her a look. She didn't mind her family seeing her in an occasional emotional state, but she'd like to keep the strong image she had created.

Ron also looked up quickly, but for quite a different reason. He saw the doctor's shadow in the hallway. He had stopped to listen to what was said about him.

Ron slipped out the side door onto the veranda, and was waiting at the doctor's car for him. "What's up, Doc?" Ron said, but not in a friendly way. "What's your story?"

Fleming stopped and nonchalantly smiled and nodded. "Yeah, I've got a story. But I'm not going to share it in there. I'm not going to share it with *The Insiders*. But maybe…" He left the words hanging and climbing into his car and drove away.

Ron returned to the library through the same door he left by.

Antoinette was still talking. Whether she was trying to make everyone forget what Ron had said earlier, or was really suspicious of Dr. Fleming, Kat couldn't tell. She was standing in an odd angle and Kat couldn't see her face. But Ron could, and he wasn't smiling.

"I know the doctor's mixed up with all this somehow." Antoinette persisted. "Maybe he's the one that's been pulling the strings. I know he certainly knows how to manipulate. He probably knows every little thing about the case and the people around it! What a perfect way to keep updated on this case—coach Ron how to get people to talk. I know *he knows* how to get people to talk about things they don't want to! To say way more than they meant to!"

Antoinette's eyes widened and looked like she had just done that very thing. She gathered her composure and quickly changed direction, "And come to think about it, I heard him and Jack talking about the new treatment center he's planning. That takes big bucks! No one is above the greed disease."

The silence was thick. Kat was furious at her aunt and she knew she should say something. But what? Ron stood and she thought he was coming to her rescue. She was wrong.

"Well, it's been a long day," Ron began, "but it's too early to call it a night. Kat has been saving something special for you. Perhaps this is a good opportunity. How about it, Kat?" Ron asked turning his back to everyone but Kat, he mouthed "Please?"

"So, he's not rescuing me after all," Kat thought. "He's got an agenda. Oh… he is probably trying to avoid the Insiders getting restless again, and demanding to go home." Getting on her feet she smiled and tried to sound like she knew what Ron was talking about. "Well, yes. I have been saving this for the right time… but I guess there's no time like the present." Pleased that The Insiders' interest had been piqued, she smiled again and recapped some of the points covered previously; wandering around subjects and events until she landed on one that seemed logical to address and that she could fill in some time with while also rekindling The Insiders' interest in the case. "During The Game in the amphitheater, as well as our discussions, you've recognized most of the names. However, there are some that I'm sure most of you are unfamiliar with.

118

Samuel Spears, Carolina Jane, and Contessa for instance. And we've heard about journals and documents that have things to do with Mount Hannah as well as the *inn* we are *in* right now." Kat said the last sentence in such a way to evoke a laugh and succeeded. "And since we're sitting here in the library at Crossroads Inn Time, I thought I'd introduce you to the man who first built it to be a stagecoach stop so many decades ago."

"Yes!" Ron beamed, and again turning so only Kat could see his face, he mouthed, "You're amazing!" Then turning to face The Insiders, he said enthusiastically, "Captain Samuel Spears' journal is one of the most exciting and moving journals I've ever read! We don't have it here tonight…"

Ron was cut off by John who asked, "Ron, sorry to interrupt, but does this have anything to do with what is going on now? I mean with Little Jimmy, Kat, and all the arrests that were made last night?"

Before Ron could answer that question Theo added "And is he somehow related to you? Is that how you ended up as heir to Crossroads Inn, Ron?"

Grinning, Ron replied, "Yes to both questions. Everything's relative—indeed." Ron chuckled at his own joke. "But nothing that will compromise the investigation and recent arrests. It is though, a story in itself! So, we won't go into it tonight because it would take all night." Ron chuckled again, as Kat walked over to stand next to the fireplace. So, I suggest in the morning, after a sunrise hike to overlook the inn and the lake and wake up with Konocti, we'll see if maybe we can make sense of all the bloodlines and connections researched and uncovered by Kat, LJ, and his dad.

"Oh, and for those who'd rather not take the hike to the top, I've asked James and Sal to set up their closed-circuit TV so you can watch the sunrise from the comfort of the library." This brought sighs of relief from Mrs. Capra and Lydia. And yes, Lenny.

Catching Catarina's eye, Ron continued, "Looks like Catarina wants the table cleared, so why don't we all move closer to the fireplace to hear Kat tell us about Captain Samuel Spears' journey from Ireland to Lake County."

As the Insiders moved towards the fireplace seating area, Ron added, "Although we won't be going into Sam's bloodline and connection to me tonight, I will say that you are in for an exciting treat. Sam was an interesting guy; in fact, a break-in by someone trying to steal Sam's journal and other documents started the investigation that led to last night's arrests." This piqued the group's interest and they quickly settled in for a listen.

PART TWO

CHAPTER FIVE

**NO TIME LIKE THE PRESENT
TO RETURN TO THE PAST**

JOURNALS ARE OPENED

When all the Insiders were seated comfortably around Kat, the younger ones on the floor, Kat smiled at Ron and this time took him by surprise and put him on the spot with, "Well, although I have come to learn about and love Cap'n Sam as he was called, I think it only right that Ron tell you about him, since the Cap'n is his great, great grandfather." Kat walked over to take Ron's place next to Mrs. Capra.

Although Ron never liked speaking in front of a crowd, except for issuing orders to calm them down he was actually excited to share his Captain Sam Spears with the insiders. "Well, let's see," Ron cleared his throat and began. "Of course, I heard the name Samuel Spears growing up. But I really didn't get to know him until I read his writings. I didn't know what an exciting life he lived or how brave and honorable he was."

Clearing his throat again and standing a little bit taller, Ron continued, "Like Kat said, my great, great grandfather was known as Captain." Smiling fondly, Ron corrected himself, "Actually, it was Cap'n.

"Samuel Spears was the middle child and second son of his father, William Spears. You may not know how things worked back in the eighteen-
121

hundreds, but the largest portion of an estate would automatically go to the eldest son. Daughters were given a dowry upon marrying, but no inheritance. That would change, but in Sam's time, to leave an estate to a daughter or a different son took an extensive bit of legal work and documentation.

"Now if the estate was large, most likely all the sons would have an inheritance, and never have to worry about accumulating money; only managing wisely, it was hoped, what they had been given in order to pass on to the next generation's male. However, if the estate was smaller or had been mismanaged, the second son and so on would be taken care of as well as the estate allowed… or size of the estate. In other words: '*MONEY*!'" Ron chuckled and his audience joined in.

As the room quieted, Ron continued, "The money would be spent on obtaining the second son a position of some sort—the military, or sometimes at sea—as a way for the son to make his fortune to establish him in life. If there were more sons, more positions would be purchased from the estate, but the majority of the estate would go to the eldest son to maintain the house. He was considered responsible to assure the house remained intact. Some of the so-called houses were three- to four-stories, housing not only the family but up to a dozen servants. Lots of mouths to feed and more than likely a multi-peaked roof to maintain. And of course, the grounds, which could be hundreds, even thousands of acres. Did I mention that even in wealthy families, if there were several sons, by the time it came around to the youngest, money would more often than not, be all spoken for?"

"What would he do then?" tender-hearted Angel wanted to know.

"Well, I'm glad you asked," Ron smiled ironically. "He would go into the cloth, as they called it. The Church." Coughing a bit to express his feelings on the subject, Ron continued: "The Clergy."

"Ha!" John blurted, "Not a very noble reason to choose that line of work." Then thoughtfully added, "But then, money still tends to be the motivating factor today." This brought more ironic laughter and scoffing from The Insiders.

"So, getting back to Samuel Spears. What was commonly called 'The Blight' had not taken a toll on the cash flow of the Spears' estate yet, so upon reaching the proper age of setting out to make his fortune, Sam's father purchased the navigator position on a ship, and was still able to set aside a large dowry for his only daughter, Caroline Jane Spears.

"This seems an appropriate time to introduce the scoundrel of the family. Every family has one, and Sam's family had a doozy! The eldest son, Donnell Spears. The meaning of his name 'Master of the World' did not go unnoticed by Donnell, which I'll explain in detail later.

"Sam, however was a hard worker and fast learner and worked his way up from ship's navigator to the rank of captain of his very own ship, and sailed into most every major port around Europe, and his final cruises were to and from America from Italy.

"It was his last cruise that was of most interest to this case, although I might mention that he made some very interesting contacts on previous

123

trips—Abraham Lincoln just to name one. Sam had visited Lincoln at his Illinois home and had even attended the man's wedding. And later when president, Lincoln offered Sam a very lucrative position as a military scout to investigate a particular problem. By now the European economy had tanked due to The Blight, and so Sam was disappointed that the fortune he had set sail to earn was slow to accumulate. He had a sister with a young child who counted on what he could send her, as Sam's brother-in-law's estate was hit hard by The Blight.

"So, Sam made the decision to leave the sea and become a 'scout' and move to America to travel the Wild West in what would be, what we would call, an undercover assignment for President Lincoln and answer directly to him." Ron paused which gave his audience time for it all to sink in and make appreciative remarks, while Ron beamed with pride!

"So how is it that no one in your family told you about this remarkable part of your family history?" John asked.

"No, no one told me. My dad died when I was young. Maybe my mom was saving it to tell me when I was older. And then she… my mother died suddenly." Ron cleared his throat before continuing. "I only found out when Kat and I retrieved the trunk she had left for me in the attic and we read his letters to his sister, Caroline Jane. I would read a letter from Sam then Kat read a correlating one from Caroline."

Kat, who as everyone knew by now could not pass up an opportunity to tell an interesting story, or even just add to it, cut in: "But it was hard to find letters written that went with the one from Sam due to the mail system and communications at the time.

124

So, what Sam didn't know was… his dear sister, Caroline Jane Spears O'Shay, along with her daughter, Celina McKenzie, was traveling to Italy to meet his ship to go to America with him. Sam and Caroline's father had been poisoned and soon after that, their mother died. The eldest son had been disinherited because of his depraved lifestyle and for not standing up to care for the girl who was carrying his child, so Sam was now heir of the Spears' estate. Then Caroline's own husband, Dylan O'Shay, and father-in-law, Captain Conor O'Shay, had also been murdered by Caroline's eldest brother, Donnell Spears who also stole all the documents along with Caroline's dowry, leaving her to be evicted by her dead husband's evil brother, Aiden O'Shay, who had stolen the documents of entailment of the O'Shay estate as well. Needless to say, Aiden O'Shay and Donnell Spears were birds of a feather. Point is, all the needed documents to prove the O'Shay estate now belonged to young Celina McKenzie and the Spears estate now belonged to Samuel Spears were stolen."

Kat had to catch her breath but she just had to get the last of it out, "The saddest part is that Caroline had unintentionally poisoned herself by packing her dead husband's favorite food, though she normally didn't eat it. She felt it would comfort her to eat foods that he had last eaten. She had also packed for her young daughter her favorite food, hoping to make the journey easier for the young girl. Unbeknownst to Caroline Jane, at the time, her brother-in-law, Aiden O'Shay, poisoned her husband's food, just as he did his own father's. And as Sam's ship drifted into the harbor, Caroline… "

Kat's words were choked by emotion, so Ron picked up the story, "Caroline begged a young Italian girl waiting on the dock to take her daughter, money, and documents and deliver them to Samuel Spears, who was already on the ship sailing to America. However, the young girl didn't understand the dying Caroline's words completely, and took the money and bought third class passage for herself and promised the purser that she would work in the kitchen to pay for the young Celina McKenzie's passage to America, where she hoped to comply with Caroline's wishes and deliver the girl, and documents to her brother. Contessa didn't know the man she would spend the next almost dozen years searching for was the captain of the very ship that carried herself and her young charge to the New World."

As most of the ladies in the library dabbed their eyes, Kat recovered enough to take the story from there, as she knew her husband would skim over unpleasant yet pertinent details. "Though Caroline didn't recognize the young girl of fourteen, she was carrying Caroline's niece. Yes! Her brother Donnell Spears' child. The girl's name was Contessa and she had worked in the Spears estate as a kitchen maid. And she *did* recognize Lady Caroline. Contessa didn't understand the Celtic writing on the documents, but she did understand that they were valuable and fully intended to keep her promise to the dying Lady Caroline Spears O'Shay. Contessa was afraid the documents might get lost or stolen since she and her charge had to bunk in the lower part of the ship; a large open area with the other third-class female passengers. So, in the darkness of night, she carefully sewed them between a slip and her dress to keep them safe. She spent a good portion of her days getting sick over the rails of the ship, hoping onlookers would think she was seasick. However, a wealthy couple made her acquaintance and offered her large tips when she delivered food to their cabin. Then one day the woman asked Contessa when her baby was due. The young girl could no longer hide her condition with the larger ill-fitting clothing in which she left the house where she worked. She was happy to have a listening ear and sympathy for the situation she found herself in. The woman, Mrs. Myers was her name, promised to help her when the time came—which came sooner than Contessa thought. Mr. Myers even paid the child's passage so Contessa could sit on the deck during the day watching Celina McKenzie play and dance instead of working in the kitchen, and delivering food to rich people.

"Mrs. Myers kept her promise and played midwife and delivered a healthy baby boy. She watched the baby and Celina McKenzie so Contessa could recover from giving birth. Then as the ship drifted into the New York Harbor, by way of fear-mongering and coercion, the Myers convinced Contessa to let them walk off the ship with the baby so, the authorities wouldn't ask questions. At the last minute, when she saw them trying to take Celina McKenzie's hand and pull her with them, she pulled the child to her side and told them to give her baby back. But they rushed down the gangplank. Celina lost them in the crowd but caught up to them as they were getting into a fancy carriage. They said they got a birth certificate that was signed by the ship's

127

captain that listed their names as parents and said he was now legally theirs. They ordered Contessa to stop screaming or they would have her arrested and both she and Celina McKenzie would be sent to an orphanage." Looking at Ron, momentarily too emotional to speak, "So, both Celina and Cap'n Spears spent the night in a new country and city. Sam in a posh hotel, but Contessa and Celina McKenzie somewhere hiding in a dark alley hungry and cold. The next day Contessa found work cleaning a hotel. The owner agreed to let her sleep on the floor of the dining room adjacent to the saloon after it closed. One night she heard a conversation coming from the saloon about Cap'n Sam Spears. She learned that he had spent the night in the very hotel she had been working in, and that he had gone to Washington D.C. As soon she had saved enough money to buy clean clothes for both herself and Celina McKenzie, she set about looking for a position in a home.

"That's how Contessa met a Mrs. Logan who was in quite a state, having just lost a maid. The socialite was having a ladies' luncheon and was shorthanded. She agreed to hire Contessa on the spot and allow her to keep Celina McKenzie with her, as long as she didn't get in the way. The childless woman took a fancy to the beautiful red-headed Celina McKenzie, who was a good-natured well-behaved child. And other than her ladies' luncheons, Mrs. Logan had nothing to do but be entertained by Celina McKenzie. Everything went smoothly— Contessa working in the kitchen, Celina playing in the garden or dancing for Mrs. Logan, until one day Celina came running to get Contessa. It seems Mrs. Logan had lost another servant who had run away with her male servant to find their fortune in California, and was hysterical!"

"That, by the way, is why the men of the house were absent." Ron interrupted.

"Oh, yes! That's a very important detail. Thank you, Ron." Kat smiled before continuing to tell how Celina had pulled Contessa to the aid of the hysterical Mrs. Logan who was only an hour away from a ladies' luncheon with no lady's maid to help her with her hair, and dress. Contessa jumped at the opportunity—though not having work experience, she did have experience doing her own hair, as well as keeping Celina McKenzie's hair done in a proper lady's hair style. "Mrs. Logan was so pleased she promoted Contessa on the spot saying, 'A kitchen maid is much easier to find than a good lady's maid.'" Kat said chuckling.

"Soon the menfolk returned from California and life in the Logan household was no longer simple. With the men came dinner parties with important associates of Mr. Logan, which did not please Mrs. Logan since she rarely enjoyed entertaining their wives. But she aimed to please her husband, so she did what was required. However, she longed to have another ladies' luncheon with the women whose company she missed.

"Many times, the dinner parties were so big that Contessa would be needed to help serve. It was during one of these meals, I believe, that she once again heard the name Samuel Spears. She learned he had indeed gone to Washington D.C. She immediately started making mental plans to leave the Logan household and take her charge to find the girl's uncle. However, she also got the news that Mr.

129

and Mrs. Logan would soon be parents. She knew she had to stay with the emotional Mrs. Logan until the birth of her child. She hoped having a baby would soften the blow of losing a lady's maid. It didn't. To the spoiled Mrs. Logan, not even the birth of a son was more important than having someone to do her hair and dress her. Protest as she would, Contessa wouldn't give in. She was determined to deliver Celina McKenzie to her Uncle Sam Spears."

This time it was Ron who butted in, "But when she arrived in Washington D.C., she found she was too late. Sam had finished his assignment and resigned his commission and had left for St. Louis, where he would be joining a wagon train heading west. While Contessa had been working and saving while following leads to find Sam, he had been living a life right out of the old Wild Western movies! He'd been leading a group of convicts disguised as men struck with gold fever and traveling with a wagon train to California; all the while helping fight off attacks from, to all appearances, wild Indians. Sam would learn that it was in fact white men dressing as Indians to keep settlers out of their territory—but I won't go into the reasons, nor the political reasoning of the president to not send troops to arrest and bring them to all justice!" Ron was clearly angered by the injustice.

"Alrighty then. Getting back to our story of Sam," Kat said grinning at Ron, "it turns out that while traveling with the wagon train along with his troop of convicts who were released from prison on the condition of riding with Sam while he investigated the so-called Indian uprising by tribes who were previously peaceful, he had the unpleasant duty of trying to keep two brothers, who were regretfully among the convicts under his command, from bullying the men and harassing the females on the wagon train."

Kat had to stop to take a breath, feeling a little embarrassed at how emotionally caught up she was getting in telling the story. Having steadied her voice, she continued in almost a whisper, "Then one evening while circling the camped wagon train to secure the area, he came upon the two scoundrels who had just caught an Indian maiden and were about to assault her. Sam pulled his gun, took theirs and sent them off into the desert on foot. The Indian maiden ran away, but Sam found she had taken his heart with her; and after finishing his assignment he quit his job with the government and was setting out to attach himself to yet another wagon train headed west. He was determined to find the Indian maiden," Kat sighed.

Ron laughed at his sentimental wife and took the story back, "You missed the part where Contessa, while working in another hotel in St. Louis, found herself under the same roof as none other than Donnell Spears, Sam's brother and the father of the boy she had given birth to on the ship. Thinking Donnell had followed her to America after all, Contessa went to his room later that night when Celina McKenzie was asleep and after the ruckus over his big win at the poker table. Donnell had won a large amount of cash and valuable documents in the card game, and the loser made all kinds of threats. But things quieted down and she anxiously went to Donnell's room. However, her hopes were once again dashed when Donnell laughed in her face and

131

turned around and actually drew his gun and pointed it at her. Somehow, she ended up with his gun and hearing a gunshot and seeing him slump to the floor, she thought she accidently shot him, but the bullet came from behind Contessa and was shot over her shoulder, mortally wounding Donnell Spears. Contessa was able to hide before a crowd gathered and the doctor was sent for.

Donnell evidently knew his brother was in town and sent for him. In the presence of the sheriff, he gave all the documents and cash he had won to Sam, and with his dying breath told him to take revenge on the person who shot him. The sheriff heard him and told Sam matter-of-factly that witnesses had come forth identifying the killer as the loser in the card game. He told Sam that a mob took the matter in hand with a lynching, so there'd be no trial.

"Looking over all the documents given to him by his brother, Sam knew that his father must be dead. He also saw by the O'Shay documents that Caroline's father-in-law must also be dead. He wondered how it was that his brother had them. One thing he was sure about: they *were not* honestly obtained. His brother was by all accounts *a no-account*." Kat looked at The Insiders and Ron, "I'm sorry… I couldn't help myself," laughed Kat, feeling the need to lighten the mood.

Ron tried not to laugh as he took the story back. "So, Contessa learned that Sam was in town, but she hid because she didn't want him to know she was there. She still believed she shot Donnell. So once again she looked for and found work. This time in the kitchen of a boarding house. She promised that

132

her charge would not get in the way, and that she would make herself useful. Which she did.

"Besides gathering eggs, picking flowers, and working in the garden, Celina McKenzie continued entertaining people with her dancing. Even earning more tips than Contessa, so the needed money was saved much faster than Contessa dared to hope. She hired a wagon and team of horses to make the trek west to follow Sam. This time they enjoyed a fond farewell from the owner and guests at the boarding house, and off they went to join a wagon train headed west.

"And this time she wasn't traveling blind, because she knew exactly where Sam was headed. She heard the commotion after Donnell won the documents. One document was a deed to a mountain in Lake County, California."

Kat once again jumped in, "The unfortunate, no! *Tragic thing*! The two bullies, named Dakota and Dusty Roads, that had terrorized the first wagon train Sam was on, and whom Sam had sent out into the desert, had joined up with the one Contessa and Celina McKenzie were on and continued their bad behavior. Seems they easily signed on with the passing wagon train. Gunslingers were welcomed by wagon masters for additional protection from marauding Indians. Contessa tried to stay out of their way, because a young woman traveling alone with a small girl wouldn't go unnoticed by them. And sure enough, she was soon targeted by the villains. An older Italian woman was traveling with her husband, and she befriended Contessa—sort of. Mrs. Lombardi looked down on Contessa, having pegged her as a house servant. Not wanting her to look down

133

on Celina McKenzie she told the snooty woman that she was Miss Celina McKenzie's nanny and that Celina was born a 'Lady' in a large Irish estate, and that her parents died from influenza and she was traveling with her to deliver her, along with valuable documents, to her uncle who was a wealthy sea captain.

"Contessa would soon come to regret bragging to Mrs. Lombardi. The Lombardi's were friends of Dakota and Dusty.

"One day Contessa had another surprise. She saw someone whom she never expected to cross paths with again. Mr. Myers! She followed him to his wagon. She couldn't resist trying to see her child. She was surprised at how much he'd grown. But there was no mistaking him as the beautiful boy she gave birth to on the ship. From then on, almost every evening after singing Celina to sleep, she would sneak over to the Myers' wagon, keeping to the shadows to go unnoticed, where she knew they would be sitting by the fire and her son would be playing with other boys from the wagons. But one tragic night when she got back, Dusty was in her wagon going through her things and Celina McKenzie was gone. 'Where is she?' she screamed, and he sneered that she ran into the desert.

"Contessa ran into the dark night calling her name but her attempts to find Celina McKenzie were abruptly ended when one or both scoundrels caught up with her and tackled her to the ground knocking her out. That is not all they did.

It was Mrs. Lombardi who found her and helped her back to her wagon and told people she had tripped in the dark while searching for the missing child. A search party went out, but not finding the girl, the wagon train moved on as scheduled, leaving Contessa to search alone. Contessa was picked up unconscious and near death by the next wagon train and taken to San Francisco, where she, once recovered, again found work. This time it was just her," Kat said sadly, her voice trailing off.

After a moment, Ron picked up where Kat had left Sam. "Captain Sam had already left the wagon train in the desert and he did in fact find his Indian maiden. After assuring her father that the wagon massacre matter was all settled, and he had reported the truth about who was attacking the wagon trains and assured him there would be no trouble by the white men, he asked for the maiden's hand in marriage. The happy father agreed to the union if she was agreeable to it. She was. So off they went to the nearest town and Justice of the Peace.

Because of the prejudice of the times, Sam bought her new clothes fit for a 'lady' and gave her a new name, Betsy Robinson Spears. But in private he always called her by her Indian name, Cat Dancing.

"Soon afterwards, the newlyweds came across an injured girl lost in the desert. She had had a head injury and couldn't speak at first or remember who she was. Sam called her Carolina Jane, after his beloved sister, and they continued west, with the girl riding behind Cat Dancing. Cat Dancing led them to Native American trails. Sam and his new wife, Cat Dancing, took the girl with them to San Francisco where Sam made inquiries about any reports of anyone losing a girl in the desert. There were none, and Sam found no notices in the post office of the bustling town, so Sam decided to adopt her legally

135

and went to court. The hopeful family was ambushed by the Lombardi's, who stood up and accused Sam of only wanting the girl because she was heiress to a fortune. They said she belonged to them and that they lost her in the desert. They said they were her family. As the judge was considering the matter, the scoundrel Dakota stood up from the back of the courtroom yelling 'She's an Injun!'

"That angered the prejudiced judge, since Cat Dancing was dressed as a white woman and Sam called her Betsy. The judge released the terrified girl to the Lombardi's, while Sam showed his identification and papers to prove that Dakota was a fugitive who had been in Sam's custody and did not fulfill his obligation of riding with him to protect the wagon train and demanded the judge arrest him and send him back to the military prison. The judge ordered it to be done however, his brother Dusty slid out the side door and escaped." Once again Ron's emotions were getting the better of him. This time it was anger! Anger at what his great, great grandparents went through. What Carolina Jane was about to endure at the hands of the evil Lombardi's. And the inexcusable prejudice that permeated the new country that was called 'a melting pot!'

Trying to cover for her husband, Kat took over, "A heartbroken Sam and Cat Dancing continued on to Lake County, having had nothing but bad experiences in San Francisco. Their journey took them on a ferry crossing the bay and many overnight layovers at stagecoach stops, Cat Dancing passed the time reading the heart-tugging journal that Sam had urged Carolina Jane to work on in order to try to remember her past. They found it among the child's

136

clothing when they returned from the courthouse to the hotel where they had been staying. "Each night when the couple stopped for the night, Sam scribbled notes in his journal, while Cat Dancing read the child's journal. By the time they reached the Midtown stagecoach stop, which was later changed to Middletown, not only had Sam come up with a plan but the couple had also learned from the journal that Carolina Jane had started getting her memory back. They also read her sweet words of the love she felt for the both of them. That journal never left Cat Dancing's possession, which is why we discovered it in a secret compartment of the trunk which Sam had purchased in San Francisco to hold the fine dresses he bought for Cat Dancing and Carolina Jane.

"Sam laid out his plan to his wife. He had obtained a land grant for a piece of property as part of his cover when traveling incognito with the wagon train. Having checked a map, he determined that it would better suit his plan than the rugged wilderness that he was also the new owner of, courtesy of his deceased brother, Donnell. And that is how he came to build Crossroads Stagecoach Stop… which later had been expanded to the Crossroads Inn where we sit right now," Kat smiled. "In fact, we are sitting in the room where Cap'n Sam's journal was found behind that wall," she said pointing to a wall which still had an outline where a sampler had hung for about a hundred years.

Ron once again took over the telling of his grandfather's story, determined this time to control his emotions, "Sam's plan was working out nicely for his bride and himself. After building the house and barn, he maintained and managed the business while

Cat Dancing preferred staying in the kitchen, where she learned to make Sam's favorite Irish meals as well as making her family's recipe for Fry Bread, which she served with beans. The stagecoach stop was building a good reputation as a place for travelers to stay and eat and had quite a following. Everything was going as planned. That is until they had another encounter with Dakota, who had somehow avoided going to prison. Sam caught him sneaking around the barn and house. He captured him and tied him up and sent for the sheriff."

CAROLINA JANE AND CELINA MCKENZIE —ONE AND THE SAME

Ron continued, "While waiting for the sheriff, Dakota very much enjoyed telling Sam that the girl he found in the desert was in fact his niece and that her mother, Sam's beloved sister Caroline, had died. Sam controlled his temper when Dakota scoffed at him for not recognizing his own niece on the ship that he was captain of. But when Dakota broke out in an evil laugh, Sam totally lost it and almost killed Dakota, but Cat Dancing stopped him. The sheriff came and Sam showed his credentials and let him know he would follow up to make sure Dakota was turned over to the military as per the law.

"Everything soon went back to their routine with the stagecoach stop and things were going well for the couple until one morning a traveler raised a ruckus about being served food that an 'Injun' cooked. It was only as he was leaving and he raised his hat and sneered that Sam recognize him to be Mr. Lombardi. Needless to say, after that ugly incident, stagecoaches passed them by and business fell off.

"Sam had heard that the Cobb Mountain area was not as prejudiced, so he decided to board up Crossroads and check out the Cobb area called Mount Hannah, which he held the deed for. Upon arriving there, he built a small cabin for Cat Dancing and himself. Soon he and Cat Dancing had befriended the post master's wife, who was herself a Pomo Indian. She seemed to know about them and the property Sam had acquired. 'There's people here you should watch out for,' was all she said.

"As it turns out, Dakota, who had been working for the Lombardis and who also had a cabin on Cobb Mountain, knew much more about the documents Sam had than Sam did, though Sam didn't have a clue how that came about. And though Sam and Cat Dancing had hoped to live on the mountain in peace, that obviously was not going to happen.

"And it all came to a head when Sam had a run-in with a Mr. Logan, who was brother to the man that lost the documents to Donnell. He claimed the land was his regardless of the documents Sam may have, and ordered him to take his squaw and leave. Sadly, they found Cobb Mountain area to be as prejudiced as everywhere else, and Sam decided to take his wife back to where they could live peacefully with her people.

"But first, he wanted to bury the documents because he knew he was being followed and feared since Logan, Dakota, and Lombardi knew of the valuable documents, one of them might try to steal them. Though Sam didn't know why, for some reason they also thought he had a fortune he had obtained while at sea. Again, how they knew he'd been a sea captain was beyond him.

"Although Cat Dancing was pressing to leave, Sam was trying to think of where he could safely bury the documents. Cat Dancing finally told him that she was pregnant and wished to be with the tribe of her people, who were in Missouri, when she gave birth. Sam was so happy, he made immediate plans to leave.

Sam landed on the perfect location to hide the documents; but suddenly, the formerly hateful and obnoxious Mr. Logan became amicable, saying he'd heard he was leaving and as a token of apology and friendship, he offered to let Sam leave anything he didn't want to take at that time, buried under a monument he had purchased for him. Sam pretended to do just that, but first carved a 'curse' with clues on the monument. He'd hoped that if Carolina Jane, whom he now knew was his own niece, Celina McKenzie, ever saw it she would figure out the clues. Then he left Cat Dancing with the one friend she had made in California, Rena, the post master's wife, while he returned to Crossroads one last time to pull a board off the wall and hide the documents and his journal there. And that's where James and Sal found them a century later."

The library was quiet and thoughtful for a few moments.

"And of course," Catarina breaking the silence, "we found Cap'n Sam's journal when we were renovating the adjacent room. But didn't think to look further. We were excited to find it, but we had a deadline to get the inn up and running... we were busy with the restoration and remodel. To think, we've had it on display in this very room for years! But well, we've been so busy with the day-to-day running of the inn that we never actually read it. That is until someone tried to steal it. Only then did we recognize the connection to the case Ron and Kat were investigating so we turned it over to them."

Ron nodded and smiled in gratitude, "That journal meant a lot to us. It not only answered so many questions but let us know there was so much more to find. And of course, I was happy to learn more about my heritage. But, Catarina and Eduardo, I want to assure you that as soon as all this is settled, I'll be happy to have it on display here in the library again."

"Yes, Sam's journal was *the key*!" Kat excitedly exclaimed. "As we searched for, found, and read all the journals and letters, it seemed a hundred years of Lake County history unfolded for us. It was as if the tremors dislodged and separated the documents and journals so they were found as we needed them." Kat laughed at herself for sounding like such a romantic. "And of course, there were additional letters and documents found later. When Sam picked up Cat Dancing on Cobb Mountain, prior to leaving for Missouri he gave Rena a forwarding address and two letters, one for Celina McKenzie O'Shay, aka Carolina Jane Spears, and one for Miss Contessa Carloni; both with security questions to answer before releasing them. And only if they answered correctly was Rena instructed to give the letters to them."

"Did they ever get the letters? Did Sam ever find Carolina Jane… I mean Celina McKenzie? Did they ever meet?" Angel pleaded to know.

"Yes, whatever became of that poor sweet girl?" Cassandra pressed for details.

Everyone seemed to have settled in on one story or another and wanted more explanations. Even Lenny had questions, "What about that crooked attorney as being the same crooked attorney that ripped off his wife and took off with the mob's money? How'd you nail him?"

Kat winked at her uncle teasingly, "Well, these are all legit questions. And we will be happy to answer *most* of them,"

"Tomorrow!" Ron laughed, and raised an eyebrow at the scowling Lenny to remind him that they couldn't discuss any of the current case. As the groanings started he added, "Look at the time for crying out loud! Even cops and P.I.s need their sleep." He laughed motioning to the sleepy-eyed Jack, who was about to fall off his chair.

Kat laughed and added, "Not to mention mommies!" giving an exaggerated yawn.

Ron and Kat gathered up Baby Ronnie and all the baby paraphernalia, except what they could leave in the upstairs bedroom that Catarina had designated a nursery. He had been sleeping under the watchful eye of a state policewoman sent by Bill Norris.

As Ron drove his family home, he looked at Kat, not for the first time, in amazement. "You're something, Kat Simmons. That was genius! You had them eating out of your hand. They aren't going to want to leave the inn until you tell them the entire story."

"You just wait a moment, Mr. Man," Kat looked at Ron sternly. "You mean 'We!' Until *we* tell them the entire story! You're going to be there with me, right? You're not trying to put this all on me, and sneak away to play cop, are you Ron?" Ron knew she'd seen through his thinly disguised flattery, though he meant every word of the compliment. "I know, I know, Babe." Ron teased. "But you do know I have a job to go to, right?"

"I do, and I also know your hours and I happen to know that even when you're on call, you can get a call, text or beep anywhere in the county." Kat bantered back smiling. It felt good to flirt with Ron again. "Things are getting back to normal," she thought reaching for Ron's hand and found it in the dark Jeep without looking. They were both looking forward to another night at home, just the three of them.

CHAPTER SIX

EVERYTHING'S RELATIVE

Instead of the sunrise walk to enjoy the view, having slept in after staying awake reminiscing about the family stories told to them the night before; morning found The Insiders finishing their breakfast buffet that Catarina had waiting for them when the Simmons' arrived. Since the latest news from Bill Norris was that things were still in a legal stalemate, Ron was much relieved that no one whined or complained about having spent another night away from home. Instead, they were more like adoring fans of what was now seeming to be more of a soap opera than an investigation.

Remembering how she had hurt Ron's feelings when she took on a similar attitude, Kat decided to make it more personal by opening with, "Last night we promised to fill you in on how the bloodlines connect with what is happening today." Each of The Insiders responded with an emphatic nod and 'Yes!'

"Well, we left off talking about what was in Ron's great, great grandfather's journal and how he left letters for Ron's distant cousin. Let's see... I think that would be a cousin twice removed... not sure how that works. Anyway, the young girl lost in the desert and then kidnapped by the unscrupulous Lombardi's was Ron's cousin. And as we read Carolina Jane's first and second journals, she became very close to our hearts, as I'm sure you would all feel if you came across a journal from a relative that had gone through so much—distant or not."

This had the effect on the group gathered in the library that Kat had hoped for. Ron smiled at his wife and nodded his appreciation.

"So, I thought this morning…" Kat leaned in towards her audience as if taking them into her confidence, "There have been events going on… illegal events... right here in Lake County. Events and activities that involve people we all know. I can't divulge these events or people to you today. But…" looking up at Ron as if he were the gatekeeper she continued, "*But soon* I can…" looking at Ron again she added firmly, "and will." Then sitting up straight, Kat took in a deep breath and said, "To help you see just why these," glancing at Ron sideways, she said, "*certain events* are relevant today, you need to know the persons who started it all. So, I thought I'd start with…" Kat leaned in closer again, and her voice got even quieter, "I thought I'd give you a treat by reading Carolina Jane's second journal, so, you can get to know her as well as we do. Then I am sure you will love her as we do." This was met with enthusiasm and the group moved to the seating area around the fireplace. As Kat walked past Ron, he brushed her hand in gratitude. Although his face remained serious and stern, he was laughing inside as he thought in amazement, "Kat should've been an actress. Or maybe an attorney." He knew she not only was buying time, but she also, in less than two minutes changed everyone's attitude from bloodthirsty voyeurs to empathetic onlookers. No one in the library seemed to realize, or perhaps care, that Kat and Ron were stretching the time while waiting for the legal battles to conclude so the case could move into litigation and witnesses could be

145

questioned. No one knew that part of what Ron was doing was smoking out a few witnesses who hadn't been quite forthcoming so far. Ron knew someone had been pulling the strings—manipulating even the most dangerous villain in this case. Ron had his suspicions, but needed proof. He was certain one of The Insiders was either the puppeteer, or knew who was. And for him to smoke this person out Ron needed time. Once The Insiders left the inn, it would be much more difficult, *perhaps impossible,* to get the goods on the person behind this whole case. Not only that, but some very dangerous perps would quite possibly hit the streets again. Lives very dear to him were at stake!

Yes, Ron was very grateful for his resourceful wife's ability to calm the nerves and keep the Insiders content to be sequestered.

But there was one thing Ron was certain of. Whoever he was looking for was family. His or Kat's. He hoped for his wife's sake they were his.

CAROLINA JANE AKA CELINA MCKENZIE O'SHAY

Kat cleared her throat, and began, "So, we've already skimmed over Captain Sam's journals, and for the most part, we've heard Caroline Spears O'Shay's heartbreaking story… and Carolina Jane's *first* journal."

This created a buzz in the library as The Insiders were eager to learn all about Celina McKenzie O'Shay, aka Carolina Jane.

Kat smiled and leaned back, getting comfortable, but said nothing, making The Insiders wonder if she was getting ready to tell them a long

146

story. Or perhaps she was going to keep them hanging. When those seated in front of Kat began to show signs of restlessness, she smiled widely. "So," she began, "We've learned a lot so far, haven't we… we've learned about Ron's dear great, great grandfather, the brave and honorable Cap'n Samuel Spears. And we've come to admire the young, determined and yes, brave, Contessa. She was the one who introduced us to the adorably sweet, precocious little Celina McKenzie O'Shay in her first journal."

As the eyes and a few mouths opened wide Kat continued, "But there is much more to know about Contessa's life. Much more. But that will come later."

Kat gave a mischievous wink as if she was holding back a big secret, before continuing, "The last we heard about Carolina Jane was she had been kidnapped in San Francisco by a Mr. and Mrs. Lombardi, who Contessa had met on the wagon train and who were friends of the evil Dakota and Dusty. All of that set the stage for what happened later and we *may* find that it's relevant to all that has happened to people living in Lake County in the past… and perhaps *now*."

Ron stood up straight and looked like he was going to say something. Kat grinned at him and winked again at her audience and chuckled, "*I said perhaps*!"

Then Kat took a breath and paused again before adding with a smile, "Carolina Jane's first journal was started when she was about eleven, shortly after Sam and Cat Dancing found her, and left off a few months later as she was beginning to get

147

her memory back. And then, sadly, she was kidnapped and left us hanging… that is until we found the *second one!"* Kat grinned and held up a small book. She let it soak in that The Insiders were about to get the answers so many had asked about the little girl who lost her memory.

"And this second one was started sometime later…. I'll let *her* tell you. She was still young, as her penmanship clearly shows." Smiling, Kat held up the tiny journal opened to the beginning. "But the journal continues into adulthood." Kat again held up the final pages of the journal showing the neat penmanship of a young woman. "As she wrote, her penmanship got better, showing her age progression. She continued writing off and on for decades."

Kat paused again thoughtfully and added, "Before I begin reading, I want to mention that as I was reading this the first time, I noticed a page ended abruptly mid-sentence and I mentioned it to Ron. Upon closer examination Ron detected that there were missing pages."

Ron interjected trying to dismiss it, "The ones James had cut out," pausing to give James an encouraging nod, he continued, "as we've all heard *why*. And he did give those pages to Catarina, who lent them to me."

Missing Ron's intentions, Kat continued, "I'll let you know when we come to those pages," Kat assured her listeners as she opened the child's tiny journal and began to read the words written by the young girl… a girl first lost in the desert and found by Sam and his new bride, Cat Dancing… and just when they were becoming a happy family and she had started getting her memory back, she was kidnapped by the unscrupulous Lombardi's. The one good thing to come from that was that she realized she could understand Italian. She didn't let the Lombardis and their evil friend, Dakota, know she could understand them when they spoke Italian, and that is how she found out that they were on the wagon train from where she got lost. And they knew the young Italian woman she was traveling with. And they knew she was Irish. Carolina Jane listened as they spoke Italian about how they learned on the wagon train about a captain's treasure and how she was an heiress to a large Irish estate and money. "That is why they took me," the little girl wrote. "They wanted my money and inheritance. They planned to take me to an orphanage when they didn't need me anymore. But I heard Dakota tell Mr. Lombardi that he would take me off their hands when they found the captain's treasure."

The Insiders gasped and sat motionless, almost not breathing as Kat read the terror the young girl felt as she heard them speak of taking her to blackmail Sam and having no intention of ever giving her back, and being locked in a dark cabin with the mean Mrs. Lombardi when Mr. Lombardi and Dakota left to look for Sam.

The Insiders were in awe when they heard how Carolina Jane escaped by climbing up the chimney, burning her little hands in the process, and they all laughed when she described how she laughed to herself imagining the fat Mrs. Lombardi searching the one room locked cabin for her. And how Mr. Lombardi would be so mad at her that maybe he would hit her like she had been hitting little Carolina Jane. The Insiders laughed loudly as Carolina Jane described something flying down over her head as she ran down the dark road causing her to scream! The laughter stopped, however, as the young girl described how once she started screaming, couldn't stop. It was like all the terror she had felt since being torn away from Sam and Cat Dancing was finally finding a way out. Most of the women in the library shed tears when Carolina Jane described how she started crying and couldn't stop crying, even though her little body ached from the force of her pent-up sobs.

Carolina Jane found herself near a hotel and hid behind barrels in the back, and slept soundly until the aroma from food being cooked inside the hotel woke her the next morning. And music. She followed the sound until she found herself dancing to the music played by a street performer as a crowd of people threw coins to her.

The Insiders felt Carolina Jane's joy as she realized she had a real talent for dancing and cheered when she joined the traveling show and escaped being caught by the Lombardi's.

But when Kat read the words of Carolina Jane's memory being fully restored, and realized she was in fact Celina McKenzie O'Shay, *not everyone* in the library of Crossroads Inn rejoiced.

Kat took a breath and summarized the rest of the journal, saying Celina McKenzie continued to use the name Carolina Jane as her stage name, because she knew the only ones who would recognize that name were her Uncle Sam and Cat Dancing. She continued writing until she was grown and a famous Irish dancer, touring across the country, and finally found herself once again in Lake County.

When she had last seen Sam, he had been traveling to Cobb Mountain. When she found her way back to the little village of Cobb, she met Rena, the Native American woman that knew her uncle. The woman gave her the letter Sam left for her, telling her about Crossroads Stagecoach Stop and that he hid something behind a wall for her. Rena also told her that a young Italian woman had also shown up asking for Sam Spears shortly after Sam and Cat Dancing had left to return to the Missouri Territory.

Celina was heartbroken to hear that Sam was no longer in California. It made it even more difficult to know that she had performed in the Missouri Territory, but didn't know her uncle was there. Rena gave her an address to write to Sam, and took her to the monument where Sam had carved a coded message hoping Carolina Jane would find it and know it meant to go to Crossroads. She did.

Celina McKenzie found her way to the Crossroads Stagecoach Stop before nightfall, and saw the sampler on the wall. She recognized the stitches and style to be that of the young woman she had traveled with. Her heart leapt when she saw that Contessa had stitched a little Irish dancing girl, and knew that Contessa had seen her dance. She then stitched a grown woman dancing an Irish jig, hoping that Contessa might someday return and see that she'd been there and know she was okay.

Celina carefully pulled away the boards behind the sampler to hide her journal there, hoping Sam would someday return and find it.

She didn't find the treasure that Sam carved on the monument and thought it must still be on the mountain. But she did find a letter written by

151

Contessa to Sam and she rejoiced to know for certain that Contessa was alright and had found her way to Cobb Mountain. She had indeed seen her dance so she knew that Celina McKenzie was not lost forever in the desert.

Celina didn't stay long because, as she wrote in a postscript in the back of her journal, she was being followed and she feared it was her father's brother, Aiden O'Shay. Celina thought he had been following Contessa and her. Contessa thought he was after the documents that she promised the dying Caroline Jane Spears O'Shay to give to Samuel Spears.

Celina also said she found documents; not only the ones Sam left, but also the ones Contessa left for Sam. But she didn't take them because she was worried Aiden would steal them.

Kat closed the journal and wiping a tear from her eye, she noticed several ladies in the audience dabbing their eyes with tissues, too.

Kat gave them a moment before she said, "So, remember where Carolina Jane left off where she was reminiscing about things Contessa told her about her mother, and stopped mid-sentence? Well, *that* is where James cut the pages out."

From the back of the room Ron caught Kat's eye and frowned and shook his head.

"Well, what was cut out?" demanded Angel, and was followed by a chorus of others asking the same thing.

MORE ABOUT CONTESSA

"Perhaps I jumped the gun and should've told you

more about Contessa before. But vabbè as they say in Italy. Whatever!" Kat smoothly changed the subject. "To sum it up, Contessa had worked in the Spears' estate as a kitchen maid. She had witnessed many parties and balls held at the Spears' estate, and knew Caroline Jane was the best dancer in the county, and sought after by many young gentlemen. Contessa knew that Lady Caroline Jane Spears had chosen Dylan O'Shay, the second son of her father's best friend, Captain Conor O'Shay. Contessa was there the night pregnant Lady Caroline Jane visited her recently-widowed and mourning mother, hoping to coax her out of her depression. But her mother, who favored her eldest son, Donnell Spears, refused to see Caroline Jane. The mother died that night and the shock sent Caroline Jane into early labor and she gave premature birth to Celina McKenzie. Contessa had heard Caroline sing to her newborn baby girl, and listened wistfully to her telling the baby what her life held out for her. How she would dance so beautifully, that all the boys would want to dance with her. She told her about her own life and how she fell in love with her baby's father and how happy he would be to meet her. She also told her that there was already a dowry entrusted for her and she would be able to choose the best young man in the county, just as she herself had done.

"When only fourteen, Contessa was coerced into gathering wild herbs by Caroline Jane's mother and brother. The brother, Donnell Spears, also seduced her and she became pregnant. She was put on a train back to Italy by his mother, who in order to keep her quiet, promised that Donnell would meet her at the port and take her to America to start a new life. Somehow Donnell's father learned of it and disinherited Donnell, putting him out of the house. Donnell and his mother, who doted on him and no doubt made him the detestable man he became, had used Contessa to gather wild *poisonous* herbs. Young Contessa had no idea the plants were poisonous, nor was she privy to their murderous plot to kill Donnell's father and hide the new will. She only learned of it when she read Caroline Jane Spears O'Shay's journal on the ship. Shortly afterwards she started her own journal, using a blank one she found in Lady Caroline's belongings. And Contessa's journal is how we learned of the Spears connection to her son, and that he had been illegally adopted and raised by the Myers', who stole him from Contessa as they were departing the ship. And her journal was also how we learned about Celina McKenzie O'Shay's line to… " looking up at Ron, Kat's voice trailed off.

Ron's weak smile couldn't hide the fact he had something heavy bothering him. Taking in a long deep breath he let it out slowly before saying, "Well let's just tie up the basics…" Ron nodded for Kat to conclude for the time being.

Kat felt Contessa's story had helped accomplish what Ron and she had agreed upon earlier—keeping The Insiders interested in staying at Crossroads, and pushing them to *feel compassion* towards those whose journeys had led them to Lake County, and especially Cobb Mountain. She thought she had accomplished that for the moment and expressed to the group gathered in the library that she was feeling tired and yearned to go upstairs and cuddle with Baby Ronnie.

Though some were murmuring, it was accompanied by smiles of understanding, as The Insiders got up and went out on the veranda to stretch their legs and discuss the lives of people from the past they now felt they knew.

From an upstairs balcony where Kat sat, holding her sleeping baby, she listened to the lively conversations floating up from the veranda. All were wondering what happened to the two women they came to feel close to, Contessa Carloni and Celina McKenzie O'Shay. And they especially wondered about Contessa's son, and if he grew up to be like his wicked adopted father, or worse—his birth father.

Kat was ready for The Insiders when they returned. Holding up a journal she mustered up a warm smile, "There's someone I think you may like to get to know."

Kat's smile waned as she held up a journal.

CHAPTER SEVEN

CONTESSA'S NIGHTMARE AT MARE VISTA

WE MEET AT LONG LAST

Kat looked into the faces of those seated around the library, while Ron positioned himself to be able to watch body language and signs of stress or nervousness as Kat began to speak quietly: "Contessa knew her son, the boy the Myers' stole from her to be Mr. Myers' heir, kept a journal. She had seen it.

"Contessa had manipulated Mrs. Logan to convince Mr. Logan that the only way to get Mr. Myers to invest in his business would be to visit him on his home turf.

"But Contessa's reason was more than just wanting to go for a 'road trip', nor was it her wanting to see Mare Vista, the mansion Mr. Myers bragged so much about building, high up in the Santa Cruz Mountains. No, none of that. This was about seeing her son. To look into his eyes to see what kind of person he was becoming.

"When the party arrived at Mare Vista, The Logan's left Contessa to unpack while the couple went downstairs to have tea with The Myers.

"Instead of unpacking the Logans' trunks, Contessa snuck out in search of the nursery where she knew her son would be. She watched in the shadows and saw her son. He was writing in a book that he tucked under something when the nanny entered the room.

"Contessa watched as the nanny changed the Myers' little girl's dress and brushed and braided her hair and tied a big bow around the braid. Contessa frowned as she noticed the nanny didn't speak to the boy nor bother combing his hair. She was both angered and dismayed by the indifference with which her son was treated. But she quietly watched and waited until the nanny left the room, taking the children down for what the upper-class called 'the viewing hour.'

"Contessa entered the nursery and wandered around quietly looking at and touching her son's things before finding the book he had hidden from the nanny. As she expected, it was a journal.

"Contessa hadn't read it all, but she read enough to know he was writing about the man he was told was his father. She saw what her son was planning.

"Suddenly the boy was behind her yelling. He had returned sooner than Contessa expected, and he was furious to find a stranger reading his journal. He pulled the book from her hands and continued to yell at her.

"Contessa didn't try to calm him down. She just looked directly into his eyes, trying to see if there was any good there. The longer she remained quiet, the more enraged and louder the boy got. He caused such a stir that the nanny came running, and screamed for Contessa to get out of the nursery!

"As Contessa was turning to leave the room, Mr. Myers rushed in. He at first was stunned, but then he recognized Contessa, and called her out for sneaking in to see the boy. He sneered that she would never get him back, and threatened to have her

157

horsewhipped and thrown in jail.

"Terrified, Contessa ran to her room and grabbed her still-packed bag. But she didn't leave alone.

"The Logans were sent away as well. By what Contessa was able to read in the boy's journal, she was not surprised that the Logans did not act angry with her. She played along and acted like she didn't know why they were all getting kicked out.

"When they had returned to San Francisco, Contessa allowed Mrs. Logan, who had long been offering to '*help*' her write a letter to Sam Spears; to help her only because she needed to go to Cobb Mountain—more specifically Mount Hannah. But she had already written one, which she would mail in its place. She also pretended to accept their offer to let them keep anything she wanted to keep safe in Mr. Logan's safe. But Contessa knew deep down she would never do that. She regretted ever having shared any information about Sam Spears and the documents with Mrs. Logan. But she would also not mail them. She knew she had to leave the documents somewhere safe, but she didn't know where. One thing she did know—the Logans were not to be trusted!

"Contessa was also certain about a couple of other things. She knew she had to leave America soon. *Very soon.* She also knew that she would not be leaving alone."

The Insider's mouths literally dropped at Kat's last statement. Looking at each other then back at Kat, they were at first at a loss for words.

Then the questions started pouring out. Kat

just sat sipping on a cup of tea she had let get cold. Finally, Kat said quietly, "I hear your questions, and I know you're anxious for answers. But let me just say I have one more journal that I think may answer many of your questions. Pulling it out of her bag she whispered, "It's Edgar Myers'." The Insiders were stunned… one much more than the others.

CHAPTER EIGHT

LITTLE BOY BLUE

EDGAR MYERS' JOURNAL

MY NAME IS EDGAR MYERS. AND THIS IS MY
7TH JOURNAL. FOR AS LONG AS I COULD
WRITE, I'VE KEPT A JOURNAL. AS A KID I
PAID CLOSE ATTENTION TO EVERYTHING
THAT WAS GOING ON AROUND ME.
ESPECIALLY WHAT MY FATHER WAS DOING.
I LOOKED UP TO HIM AND TRIED TO IMITATE
HIM.

HE KEPT A JOURNAL. I ASKED HIM WHY,
AND HE SAID ALL IMPORTANT MEN DO.
THAT'S WHEN I STARTED MY OWN. WRITING
MUNDANE THINGS LIKE WHAT I HAD FOR
MEALS OR SECRET PASSAGES I FOUND, AND
HOW I SNUCK INTO THE KITCHEN FOR
SNACKS. OR THINGS MY FATHER TAUGHT
ME OR THINGS I HEARD HIM SAY. LATER I
BECAME MORE EARNEST IN MY
JOURNALING. I WAS TRYING TO FIGURE OUT
WHY AFTER MY SISTER WAS BORN
EVERYTHING CHANGED. I WAS NO LONGER
LOVED. MY FATHER NO LONGER SPENT
TIME WITH ME, TEACHING ME THINGS I
WOULD NEED TO KNOW TO CARRY ON HIS
NAME. MARE VISTA AND HIS BUSINESS. I
WAS AS GOOD AS CAST OUT. I'VE FOUND
THE MANY SECRET DOORS, ROOMS,
STAIRWAYS, PASSAGEWAYS AND TUNNELS,
TO BE HELPFUL IN MY QUEST TO SOLVE THIS

RIDDLE. SOME OF THE PASSAGEWAYS ARE FOR THE SERVANTS, TO APPEAR AND DISAPPEAR THROUGH. SERVANTS ARE SUPPOSED TO BE INVISIBLE. NO ONE LIKES TO SEE THEM. AND EVEN WHEN THEY DO, THEY IGNORE THEM AND PRETEND NOT TO SEE THEM.

I'M NOT A SERVANT, BUT MORE AND MORE I'M TREATED THAT WAY.

BUT THE SERVANTS CAN'T IGNORE ME. SO, I GET IN THEIR WAY AND MAKE THEIR JOB DIFFICULT ON PURPOSE. THEY DO GET CROSS WHEN I GET IN THEIR WAY. BUT THEY NEVER GIVE ME AWAY. THEY KNOW THEY MUST BE NICE TO ME, BECAUSE I'VE FOUND OUT THIER SECRETS. I HAVE BEEN SPYING ON THEM EVEN LONGER THAN I HAVE SPIED ON MY FATHER.

SPYING ON THEM, LISTENING TO THEM COMPLAIN ABOUT MY PARENTS AND THEIR POSITIONS IN LIFE. THEIR STORIES AND GOSSIP, WHILE IN SEARCH OF THE MYSTERY OF WHY I AM NO LONGER LOVED.

I HAVE RATHER ENJOYED SNEAKING AROUND SPYING ON PEOPLE. BUT I AM ESPECIALLY INTERESTED IN FINDING OUT ALL I CAN ABOUT MY FATHER.

READING HIS JOURNALS AND DOCUMENTS,

HIDING AND EAVESDROPPING ON THE CONVERSATIONS AND ALL THE MEETINGS FATHER HAS IN HIS LIBRARY.

LISTENING TO ARGUMENTS WITH MY

MOTHER. WHICH I QUITE ENJOY THE MOST. IT'S MY FAVORITE. I LOVE KNOWING THEY ARE AS UNHAPPY AS THEY HAVE MADE ME. BY THE TIME I WAS A TEEN I HAD SOLVED THE MYSTERY, AND KNEW THE WHOLE STORY. I FOUND MY BIRTH CERTIFICATE SIGNED BY THE CAPTAIN OF THE SHIP THEY CAME TO AMERICA ON. CAPTAIN SAMUEL SPEARS. BUT SOMETHING ELSE. A LETTER OF ADOPTION. AS IF THAT WAS NOT SHOCKING ENOUGH, I OVERHEARD CONVERSATIONS BETWEEN THE MYERS ABOUT THEM STEALING ME SO FATHER WOULD HAVE A MALE HEIR IN ORDER TO KEEP THE MONEY LEFT FOR HIS HEIR. AND HIS NAME WOULD BE CARRIED ON. AND HOW HE BUILT MARE VISTA WITH MY INHERITANCE. MY MONEY. I COMFORTED MYSELF TELLING MYSELF THAT AT LEAST I WAS WANTED, IF NOT LOVED. AND I FELT I HAD A FUTURE. LATER I ALSO LEARNED SOMETHING ELSE. SOMETHING I WILL BE ABLE TO USE. I DON'T KNOW HOW JUST YET. BUT I AM SURE IT IS GOOD THAT I HAVE THIS INFORMATION. SOMETHING ABOUT MY ADOPTED FATHER SENDING A HIRED GUN TO GET A DEED AND DOCUMENTS FROM THE LOGANS. SOMETHING WENT WRONG THOUGH AND THE MAN RETURNED EMPTY HANDED. I HEARD THEM SPEAK OF ANOTHER MAN BEING HUNG. AND LATER MY FATHER SENT THE SAME MAN TO STALK CAPTAIN SAMUEL SPEARS, WHOM I DON'T KNOW, BUT SAW HIS NAME ON MY BIRTH

CERTIFICATE. IT SEEMS HE HAS SOMETHING OLD MAN MYERS WANTS. THE MAN WAS ALSO HIRED TO FOLLOW A WOMAN NAMED CONTESSA CARLONI, WHO I DO KNOW. FROM THE WAGON TRAIN WE RODE IN TO CALIFORIA.

MY PARENTS WERE BUSY WITH THEIR OWN INTERSTS WHILE WE TRAVERSED THE PRAIRIES AND MOUNTAINS ON OUR WAGON TRAIN JOURNEY TO CALIFORNIA. AND I BEFRIENDED A FEW BOYS WHOSE FAMILIES WERE TRAVELING WITH US. ONE NIGHT WE WATCHED A LITTLE GIRL DANCING TO A SONG HER MOTHER SANG TO HER. AFTER THAT I SNUCK BACK OFTEN TO WATCH THEM. I THOUGHT THEM BOTH VERY BEAUTIFUL. NOTHING LIKE THE FAT OLD HEN WHO CALLED HERSELF MY MOTHER. I HATED HER EVEN BEFORE I LEARNED SHE WAS NOT MY REAL MOTHER.

YES, I LEARNED THE WHOLE THING... HOW THEY TRICKED A POOR ITALIAN GIRL ON THE SHIP TO AMERICA AND STOLE ME. FUNNY THING IS I ALWAYS KNEW I WAS ITALIAN. NOT GERMAN LIKE THE MYERS TRIED TO CONVINCE ME I WAS. I KNEW I WAS ITALIAN... NOT GERMAN LIKE MY LITTLE SISTER WHOSE MOTHER WAS GERMAN LIKE THE MYERS. YES, I CAME TO KNOW THAT THE MAN I CALLED FATHER HAD SIRED A CHILD BY MY NANNY WHO DISAPPEARED SOON AFTER THE CHILD WAS BORN, AND SUDDENLY THEY HAD A DAUGHTER. MY SISTER. AND WE HAD A

163

NEW NANNY AND THE WOMAN I CALLED MOTHER WOULD NEVER ENTER THE NURSERY AGAIN. I HAD BEEN REPLACED BY A BABY WITH MYERS BLOOD IN HER VEINS, AND MYERS' WIFE HAD NO ATTACHMENTS TO THAT CHILD. AND SHE HAD NO MORE REASON TO BE NICE TO ME ANYMORE. I FOUND OUT THAT OLD MAN MYERS FORGED HIS FAMILIES' ENTAIL WHICH HAD ORIGINALLY EXCLUDED DAUGHTERS FROM INHERITING.

AND NOW I KNOW SOMETHING ELSE TOO. I KNOW MY DAYS ARE NUMBERED AT MARE VISTA. NOT ONLY AM I NOT GOING TO INHERIT IT LIKE I HAD BEEN PROMISED BEFORE GERTRUDE WAS BORN, BUT I WILL SOON BE PUT OUT. I HAD FIRST STARTED KEEPING A JOURNAL TO MIMIC MY FATHER. BUT LATER TO TRY AND FIGURE OUT WHAT HAPPENED TO MY PERFECT LIFE. AND NOW I KEEP A JOURNAL TO GATHER INFORMATION WITH WHICH I PLAN TO BLACKMAIL MYERS. AND TO GET EVEN FOR REJECTING ME AND KICKING ME OUT WHEN THAT HAPPENS. AND I KNOW IT WILL SOON.

OR MAYBE HIS PLAN FOR ME IS WORSE THAN THAT! I MUST DO SOMETHING TO BECOME IMPORTANT TO OLD MAN MYERS AGAIN. BE OF USE TO HIM.

NOW MORE THAN EVER I MUST COME UP WITH A PLAN. NOT JUST SOME WAY FOR MYERS TO HAVE A USE FOR ME, BUT A PLAN

TO DESTROY HIM AND HIS FAMILY. I HAVE NEVER HATED HIM MORE THAN I DO AT THIS MOMENT.

I MUST THINK OF A FAILSAFE PLAN. AND YES, IT'S MORE FOR A VENDETTA THAN MONEY.

I'VE KNOWN THE COMBINATION OF THE SAFE FOR YEARS, AND COULD GET MY HANDS ON MONEY ANYTIME I WANTED. I WATCHED OLD MAN MYERS OPEN THAT SAFE HUNDREDS OF TIMES, AND HELPED MYSELF A LITTLE AT A TIME AND HID THE MONEY EXACTLY LIKE I WATCHED HIS WIFE DO ALL MY LIFE.

NO, I DON'T NEED MONEY. BUT WHAT I WANT IS *REVENGE*! MAKE HIM THINK HE IS USING ME TO GET SOMETHING HE WANTS VERY BADLY AND THEN PULL IT OUT FROM UNDER HIM. MAKING HIM FALL FROM THE HIGH POSITION HE HAS STOMPED ALL OVER OTHER PEOPLE TO GET TO.

I THINK I JUST FIGURED OUT HOW TO DO THAT. FAT OLD MAN MYERS HAS TRIED TO GET CLOSE TO MR. LOGAN FOR AS LONG AS I HAVE A MEMORY. LOGAN OWNS A MOUNTAIN MYERS WANTED BUT LOGAN BEAT HIM TO IT. MYERS EVEN HAD SOMEONE KILLED TO GET THE DEED AND DOCUMENTS. BUT THAT FAILED. AND AFTER THE LOGANS' DAUGHTER WAS BORN MYERS BEGAN PLANNING ON ME MARRYING HER. ONLY BECAUSE HE WANTS A WAY INTO THEIR MONEY AND THE

165

MOUNTAIN THEY OWN. MOUNT HANNAH.

THAT IS THE ONLY THING THAT WOULD MAKE HIM WANT ME AGAIN. NOT THAT I WANT HIM TO WANT ME. I SPIT AT THAT THOUGHT. BUT I WILL TELL HIM I WILL MARRY THE LOGANS' DAUGHTER. THAT I WILL DO FOR HIM. I ALWAYS RESISTED BECAUSE SHE WAS UGLIER THAN ANYONE I'D EVER SEEN AND EVEN MORE STUPID. BUT I WILL DO ANYTHING WITHIN MY POWER TO BRING THE MYERS DOWN.

TONIGHT, I TOLD MYERS I WISHED HIS ADVICE ON A MATTER AFTER DINNER IN THE LIBRARY. I MADE KNOWN MY DESIRE AND MADE MY CASE TO HAVE THE ENTAIL RESTORED SO THAT I WOULD HAVE SOMETHING OTHER THAN THE MYERS' NAME TO OFFER MR. LOGAN WHEN I ASK FOR HIS DAUGHTER'S HAND. MYERS COULDN'T AGREE FAST ENOUGH! IN FACT, JUST AS I EXPECTED, HE BECAME JUBILANT! EVEN CALLING TO MRS. MYERS AND GERTRUDE TO JOIN US IN HIS LIBRARY—WHICH IS NOT DONE AFTER DINNER, OF COURSE. IT IS CUSTOMARILY A TIME THAT WOMEN ARE SENT TO THE PARLOR TO DISCUSS WHATEVER MUNDANE THING IS HAPPENING IN THEIR UNEXCITING LIVES AND THE MENFOLK ENJOY A BRANDY AND CIGAR AND ENJOY 'MAN TALK'. THIS WAS NEVER THE CUSTOM BETWEEN MYERS AND MYSELF. WE WOULD USUALLY GO OUR SEPARATE WAYS. I ALMOST FELT A TWINGE

OF REGRET WHEN I SAW JUST HOW HAPPY THIS NEWS MADE THE MYERS. EVEN GERTRUDE, WHO KNEW THE MATCH WOULD MAKE HER SITUATION MUCH MORE DESIRABLE. SHE WOULD BE ABLE TO PICK AND CHOOSE A SUITABLE HUSBAND OF POSITION AND WEALTH. WHEN GERTRUDE AND I WERE EXCUSED AND SENT UPSTAIRS, INSTEAD OF SLIPPING OUT THE BACK DOOR AS PER MY USUAL, I RUSHED UPSTAIRS AND AS SOON AS GERTRUDE HAD CLOSED HER BEDROOM DOOR, I SLID THROUGH THE SECRET DOOR TO THE STAIRWAY PASSAGE TO EAVESDROP ON THE MYERS' CELEBRATION WHICH WAS STILL GOING ON IN THE LIBRARY. I MADE MYSELF COMFORTABLE AND ENJOYED HEARING GOOD CONVERSATION ABOUT MYSELF FOR A CHANGE, THEN THEIR CONVERSATION DRIFTED OFF TO A DISTANT EVENING CONCERNING THE LOGANS.

WHAT I HEARD MADE ME HATE THE MYERS MORE THAN I THOUGHT I WAS ABLE TO HATE ANYONE OR ANYTHING. THEY SPOKE OF A VISIT FROM THE LOGANS WHEN THEY WERE STILL LIVING IN SAN FRANCISCO, AND A NANNY THAT ACCOMPANIED THEM TO MARE VISTA WHEN I WAS A CHILD. MY EARS PERKED UP. I REMEMBERED THAT INCIDENT VERY WELL. I REMEMBERED HER. HOW SHE STARED AT ME. SEARCHING MY EYES AS IF LOOKING FOR TRUTH, AS SHE STOOD THERE IN THE NURSERY HOLDING MY JOURNAL.
167

AND I REMEMBERED HOW VICIOUS I WAS TO HER, AND MADE SUCH A SCENE THAT SHE FLED. BUT WHAT I HEARD MY SO-CALLED PARENTS SAY TONIGHT FILLED ME WITH SO MUCH ANGER I COULD BARELY HOLD IT IN. I WANTED TO BURST INTO THE LIBRARY AND CONFRONT THEM. DEMAND OF THEM HOW DARE THEY REJECT ME, AND STILL KEEP ME FROM MY REAL MOTHER. THE MOTHER THAT RISKED EVERYTHING JUST TO SEE ME AGAIN. HOW I HATED THE MYERS FOR NOT TELLING ME WHO SHE WAS... FOR NOT LETTING HER TAKE ME AWAY FROM MARE VISTA AND THEM.

I HAVE CARRIED THAT HATRED ALL MY LIFE. YES, THE VENDETTA I HOLD IN MY HEART IS JUST WAITING FOR A CHANCE TO EVEN THE SCORE.

YES, I KNOW NOW. I'LL ADMIT IT TO MY SELF NOW. I ADMIT THAT I KNEW THE WOMAN THAT I FOUND THAT NIGHT SO LONG AGO IN THE NURSERY. I KNEW IT EVEN THEN. I KNEW WHO SHE REALLY WAS. WHO ELSE WOULD IT BE? WHO ELSE WOULD BE INTERESTED AND BRAVE ENOUGH TO SNEAK INTO THE NURSERY JUST TO READ MY JOURNAL. AND LOOK INTO MY EYES. YES. WHO ELSE WOULD IT BE BUT MY MOTHER?

MYERS' WORDS TO HER THAT NIGHT ONLY CONFIRMED WHAT I ALREADY KNEW. SHE WAS MY MOTHER.

BUT IN MY CHILDISH NAIVETY I SPENT

YEARS TRYING TO CONVINCE MYSELF THAT HE SENT HER AWAY BECAUSE HE HAD COME TO LOVE ME.

BUT I KNEW IT WAS NOT TRUE. I KNEW OLD MAN MYERS WAS ONLY THINKING OF HIMSELF AND BEING THE MEAN AND HATEFUL MAN, HE ALWAYS HAS BEEN.

AND I WAS PRETENDING THAT HE HAD ANY FEELINGS FOR ME BESIDES HATE. I KNOW AND HAVE ALWAYS KNOWN THAT FAT OLD MAN MYERS ONLY STOLE ME OUT OF GREED. HE NEEDED A MALE HEIR TO GET HIS GREEDY MITTS ON AN INHERITANCE SO HE COULD BUILD MARE VISTA AND PRETEND HE IS AS GOOD AS THE LOGANS. THAT HAS BEEN THE ONLY THING HE WANTED ME FOR.

WHEN MY MOTHER SHOWED UP HERE, HE SENT HER AWAY OUT OF MEANNESS, SELFISHNESS AND MOST OF ALL GREED!

AND HEARING HIS WORDS TONIGHT. HEARING OLD MAN MYERS BRAG ABOUT SENDING MY MOTHER AWAY AND LAUGH ABOUT TAKING ME FROM HER TWICE. WELL, THAT HAS MADE IT IMPOSSIBLE FOR ME TO GO ON PRETENDING THAT THERE IS ANY CHANCE OF THAT FAT OLD MAN MYERS EVER LOVING ME.

AND I CAN'T PRETEND ANYMORE THAT I DIDN'T KNOW SHE WAS MY MOTHER. SOMETHING ELSE I KNEW. IN MY MOTHER'S EYES IN THE WAY SHE LOOKED AT ME. SEARCHING MY EYES. I SAW SOMETHING I

169

HAVE NEVER SEEN BEFORE OR SINCE. I SAW LOVE.

AND SHE PROVED HER LOVE FOR ME THAT NIGHT.

AND FAT OLD MAN MYERS ACTS ONLY OUT OF MEANNESS AND SPITE. HE PROVED IT THAT NIGHT.

WELL, I'VE LEARNED A LOT FROM MYERS. HE'S TAUGHT ME HOW TO BE MEAN AND SPITEFUL. AND I WILL PROVE IT TO HIM ONE DAY SOON.

WELL, I HAVE CARRIED OUT PHASE ONE AND TWO OF MY PLAN. THAT OF COURTING AND BECOMING ENGAGED TO THE YOUNG AND UGLY MISS LOGAN. WHOM I MUST SAY IS EVEN HOMELIER CLOSE UP THAN THE DISTANCE I'VE BEEN ABLE TO KEEP MYSELF. SIMULTANEOUSLY, I FOUND THE MOST DISAGREEABLE AND LEAST DISIRABLE… THE VERY LAST PERSON THE MYERS WOULD EVER WISH TO BE CONNECTED TO IN ANYWAY, LET ALONE BY MARRIAGE. A BEAUTIFUL BUT POOR LOCAL GIRL WHO IS IN SERVICE IN NONE OTHER BUT THE LOGAN'S KITCHEN. YES, AND WHOM I NOT ONLY IMPREGNATED BUT ALSO, UNLIKE THE *'SPEARS GENTLEMAN'* WHO USED MY MOTHER, I SECRETLY WED THE MOTHER OF MY UNBORN CHILD. IN A SMALL WAY I FEEL I DID IT FOR MY OWN MOTHER, AS MUCH AS I DID IT TO BRING DOWN THE MYERS. I

CANNOT WAIT TO ANNOUNCE THIS FACT AT THE WEDDING THAT WILL BE HELD IN MARE VISTA. BUT I HAVE PUSHED THE WEDDING OFF UNTIL AFTER MY WIFE GIVES BIRTH. BIRTH TO A SON I AM HOPING BEYOND HOPE!

WELL, I HAVE GOTTEN MY REVENGE BUT NOT TO MY GREAT SATISFACTION. I HAVE BROUGHT SHAME ON THE MYERS FAMILY.

ON MISS LOGAN'S AND MY WEDDING NIGHT, JUST BEFORE THE CEREMONY, I MADE A FOOL OF OLD MAN MYERS BY PRETENDING TO BE DRUNK. AND IN FRONT OF THE ENTIRE COUNTY, I PROCLAIMED MY DISDAIN FOR THE UNSIGHTLY LOGAN GIRL AND SAID I WAS PUSHED INTO THIS BY *'MY FATHER'* WHO ONLY WANTED A CONNECTION TO THE LOGANS' MONEY, BUT I COULDN'T GO THROUGH WITH THE MARRIAGE BECAUSE I'M ALREADY MARRIED TO SOMEONE ELSE, WHO HAS GIVEN BIRTH TO MY CHILD. AND I PRESENTED MY WIFE, AND SON.

I THOUGHT MY HAVING A SON WOULD RIP MARE VISTA FROM THE MYERS, AND I WOULD HAVE THE PLEASURE OF GIVING THEM THEIR WALKING NOTICE. BUT IT TURNS OUT OLD MAN MYERS WAS ONE STEP AHEAD OF ME.

HE NEVER TORE UP THE FORGED ENTAIL PAPER. INSTEAD HE DESTROYED THE ORIGINAL. IT IS I, ALONG WITH MY NEW

WIFE AND SON WHO ARE BEING PUT OUT OF MARE VISTA.

I THOUGHT I COULD GO TO MY PLAN B; THAT OF COMPLETELY RUINING OLD MAN MYERS' NAME AND HIS PRECIOUS DAUGHTER AND FUTURE HEIR. I TRIED TO SELL ALL THE INFORMATION AND RECORDS OF HIS CROOKED DEALS AND SCHEMES WHICH I HAD SPENT A LIFETIME GATHERING, TO A PERSON WHO WORKS FOR A CROOKED REAL ESTATE FIRM WHOM I HAVE BECOME AQUAINTED WITH. I WAS SURE HE WOULD PURCHASE THE INFORMATION AND RECORDS AND USE IT TO BLACKMAIL THE MYERS. THE MYERS WOULD GO BROKE, AND I WOULD HAVE ENOUGH MONEY TO TAKE MY WIFE AND SON FAR AWAY. *ITALY MAYBE*.

THE INFORMATION I HAD GATHERED WOULD *INDEED* RUIN THE MYERS FAMILY REPUTATION AND QUITE POSSIBLY SEND OLD MAN MYERS TO JAIL. SO, I WAS SURE THEY WOULD PAY UP. WHAT I DIDN'T COUNT ON WAS THAT THEY HAD NO MONEY TO PAY. MYERS HAD MADE SOME BAD INVESTMENTS AND HAD PUT MARE VISTA UP AS COLLATERAL. SO INSTEAD OF GETTING MY REVENGE AND WALKING AWAY WITH THEIR MONEY, THE MYERS LOST MARE VISTA TO THE VERY LOS GATOS CROOKED REAL ESTATE FIRM I TRIED TO SELL THE INFORMATION TO. AND SOMEHOW THE LOMBARDIS ACQUIRED IT. I GET NO SATISFACTION FROM KNOWING

THEY LOST MARE VISTA, SINCE IT WAS NOT AT MY HAND.

I WILL GET MY REVENGE. I WILL! TO BOTH THE MYERS AND THE LOMBARDIS AND YES, THE LOGANS. BECAUSE NOW I AM REGRETTING NOT MARRYING THEIR DAUGHTER INSTEAD OF THEIR SERVANT. SHE HAD THE HIGHEST DOWRY IN THE STATE, SO I'VE HEARD. I COULD HAVE BEEN RICH, AND KEPT MY PRETTY SERVANT IN SECRET LIKE MOST MEN OF LARGE ESTATES DO.

The handwriting changed, and someone added a postscript to the journal:

BEFORE my husband, Edgar Myers, could be thrown out, he drank himself to death. Well, not exactly. He drank and fell down the stairs at Mare Vista. Mrs. Myers has ordered me to take my child and leave, which didn't surprise me a bit. But she hasn't forced me out yet. I'm sure it's because she knows Edgar kept a journal and she is searching for it and all the documents he stole. So, she wants all his things left alone. She has no idea I knew all about his journal, and have read it, along with valuable documents he stole from Mr. Myers' safe. I have snuck out of the house, down a secret passage Edgar showed me once. And with the bag of money Edgar has been stealing from Mr. Myers I can provide a comfortable home for my son. I only packed a bag for the baby, and of course the journal and documents. Then I snuck out through the basement with my baby boy and in case I am caught I will hide the journal and all documents from them. The secret way out of the
173

tunnel that Edgar showed me has come in handy. I used to come that way and meet Edgar in the basement before we were married. That is where I told him I was pregnant. I was relieved to see that he was thrilled instead of angry. But having read his journal, I now know why. It was not because he loved me. He never loved me. He had planned on making me pregnant all along. I have to take the money now because I must have money for my son and me to survive. I only hope I am not caught escaping and the money taken from me.

I will not chance them finding the journal and documents, which I can use to ensure my release if caught. So I am hiding the journal behind a loose stone in the tunnel drainage, and will come back for it at a later time, when I'm sure the Myers have stopped looking for me. I'm not sure what I'll do with it. There is some damning information in it for sure. Although I don't think I could bring myself to use it the way Edgar tried to. Only if I truly become destitute. I had to stop working when I became pregnant, but if I am careful with the money I found that Edgar had hidden with his journal, my son and I can live comfortably and he can even get an education.

I have to admit that just knowing that his journal and all these damning documents are here, in the Myers' beloved Mare Vista will give me sweet satisfaction for all the mean things Mrs. Myers has said to me, and called my son.

Kat became quiet, as were The Insiders. They seemed to be waiting for Kat to finish the story of the young mother. "That's all I know, except that LJ found the journal and documents when he and his dad were planning the escape route for when LJ and I would be trapped in the tunnel. They studied the journal and traced all the names and put some charts together." Kat had a faraway look in her eyes, as if she were still in the past.

PART 3

CHAPTER NINE

THE PAST HAS LED US
TO THE PRESENT

BLOODLINES AND FAMILY TIES

Seeing that Kat needed a moment to return to the present, Ron took over for her.

"So, as we've read the journals and letters, we've come to hear about four main families. The Spears', the O'Shay's yes… but also the Myers', the Logan's and the LOMBARDI family. The latter is the one family that seems to have kept ties with Lake County. Well, and then there is the Logan connection to Mount Hannah. But there is another family whose history and genes are intertwined with some of those families. The *Carloni family*.

"So okay, here it is in a nutshell. Ron started, "It gets twisted and complicated but since you asked...

"Like I said the other night—at least I think I did—Kat, LJ, and his dad, had already had the bloodline to Jimmy traced, as well as Kat's, to figure out why she was a threat to... to *certain people of suspect*. Then they researched mine to figure out who the heck the guy who was pretending to be my cousin, Dusty Rhodes, was. Turns out, he was related to Kat though her father's bloodline. But sorry to say, to me, as well, on my mother's side."

This caused raised eyebrows and a gasp from Angel, as she put her hand over her mouth.

"Yeah, I know," Ron grimaced. "That makes

176

Kat and me related in some *very, very* distant way."

Kat interjected, "And as I was about to say, LJ, his dad, and I reread all the journals and letters. Gathering names and dates, we put together bloodlines of five main families that seem to be all tied to what's been going on and… " Kat abruptly stopped, and looked questioningly at Ron.

He frowned, and said, "How about a little break. I'm thinkin' *we all* could use one. Get up, stretch your legs, and walk around a bit. Get the circulation going, then freshen up and when everyone's back, we'll see what's been happening in the kitchen that smells so good." There was a little murmuring, but no grumbling as The Insiders left the library.

Ron waited until everyone had left the library before speaking in a low voice to Kat, "I got a text from Bill. Not looking too promising. The attorneys are doing a bang-up job of twisting the facts. There's concern about an injunction being filed to disallow anything that took place here the other night into evidence. If that happens everyone will be cut loose."

Kat looked concerned and said, "I was afraid of that, so I texted Bill to get in touch with LJ and tell him we need his help. And I asked him if Jimmy could join us on an Internet conference to go over the bloodlines and family ties, and to tell him to make it long and confusing. But… "

"Yeah, if everyone leaves the inn, what's the point? I need to come up with something… " Ron was cut off by Kat's cell phone alerting her to a text.

"Oh, here's Jimmy now. What should I tell him?"

"Let's stick with your plan for now. I'll duck

into the pantry and go over our notes. I think we've missed something. Or someone. And if things go sour, I don't think it's a good idea to share the rest of the documents or journals. Better keep them under wraps for now. And by that, I mean under lock and key!"

Catarina and her staff had just finished setting up a buffet when The Insiders started trailing in. They were all engaged in various conversations about one person or another, all from the distant past. The conversations continued over lunch, and they didn't notice James and Kat in deep discussion near the large television that had appeared: the very one used the night of The Game. No one was concerned or even wondered what would be transmitted to them on it.

Kat smiled as The Insiders returned to their previous seats near the fireplace, and one by one they finally noticed the blackened TV. Kat welcomed them all back saying, "I'm so glad we took that much needed break, and how about that lunch?" Even though she herself hadn't had a bite to eat since early morning.

Kat took a long breath and carefully choosing her words began, "As Ron was saying earlier, we've traced the bloodlines of... the Spears and O'Shay families, yes... but also the Myers, the Logan and the Lombardi families. The latter is the one family that seems to have kept a constant presence in Lake County. Well, besides the secret Logan connection to Mount Hannah." She smiled again nervously glancing at Ron, while quickly adding, "by 'we' I mean LJ, his dad, and me." Using the remote control, she turned on the screen and to everyone's surprise Little Jimmy's face appeared wearing a big smile. Angel noticed right away it was a forced smile.

After being greeted by The Insiders, LJ began quickly, "So, I hear you're interested in my DNA?" The surprised audience just sat there looking at LJ and each other.

Undeterred, LJ continued, "I understand we're gonna trace the *five families* from their beginning to the present. At which point... connecting the dots points to *me*." The audience just stared blankly at the screen, Little Jimmy's demeanor seemed different. "Yep, the *heads* of the five families is where I got my start. *Explains a lot, doesn't it?*" Finally, his audience laughed a little, remembering the precocious Little Jimmy who was always in trouble. And he smiled, but his eyes remained serious. From then on it was a cake walk. Jimmy shared the screen with ancestry charts and took them down each family line until there was nowhere else to go but to him.

Angel exclaimed, "This is so cool that you are related to us, LJ. I knew there was something I loved about you!"

"So you are related to *all of us*?," James said, meaning his sisters and himself.

"That's raaaght!" LJ replied, drawing an imaginary gun and aiming it. "And I always knew there was something about *you*!," *almost* repeating Angel's line. This finally got a real chuckle from LJ's audience.

"And the *Lombardis*?" Lenny scoffed. That means you're related to my wife?" He had never felt comfortable knowing his wife was related to gangsters.

"Heeey! Uncle Lenny!" Jimmy said with his best Fonzie accent, and with his hands out palms up he shrugged, "We're *family*! What can I say?"

The room filled with laughter, partly due to LJ's joke but mostly from Lenny's reaction to it.

Despite the serious nature of the conference call and information being dispersed, Ron, who had returned to the library, couldn't help but be pleased to see this side of LJ. He rarely ever joked. Kat was just pleased he found his 'Italianness'.

Someone offscreen murmured something to LJ, and he said, "Bad news, we won't be discussing the Good Doctor Fleming's bloodline, because as we all know, his blood runs cold. Yep, he's a cold fish! For all I know, he may be *sleeping with the fish*!

"Well, folks this was fun, but seems I'm needed to *fight crime* elsewhere, so I gotta quit clowning around and get down to business." Grinning, he added, "So, I'm going to try to be serious. Starting from the top... With regard to those of you in the library... our research, as this chart makes clear, revealed that James and his sisters, as mentioned earlier, are all related to Sam Spears. And we all know Ron is also, since he couldn't stop bragging about it all summer. *Just kidding*, Ron.

"Moving on. But the guy who did the break-in that started this whole investigation who claimed to be named Dustin Rhodes, a black sheep in Ron's family, is in reality a blacker sheep in Kat's family. And deep in with the MOB, namely, Johnny Amoretti. So following the ties from Dusty Rhodes to Ron's dad as well as Kat's dad... Does that make

Kat and Ron kissing cousins? I don't know, but it all seems weird to me!"

Kat, who had long stopped laughing, gasped. "What's going on?" she asked Ron, who just shook his head, but to himself said, "LJ is deliberately mixing up my bloodline and being rude. He's trying to get my attention." Reaching for his phone he texted his stepdad.

LJ continued, "Now backing up the old dusty road a bit, we'll follow the ties from Dakota and his brother Dusty 'Roads,' who changed the spelling of his name to 'Rhodes' when he married into a respectable, but mobbed-up family; and shares DNA with *Mr. Ron Deputy Sheriff Simmons*. His wife, the daughter of said mobbed-up 'Good Guy'… oops wrong mob—this guy was in the Irish mob, and was named Logan. Yep… the very Logan who Contessa worked for back in the day—*that* Logan. Dusty and Mob Princess' union resulted in a daughter, who later married… drum roll please… Edgar Myers of Mare Vista fame, and they of course procreated to bring into the world none other than… " LJ deliberately left his sentence, and audience, hanging.

Dr. Fleming had joined the group in the library after lunch, and was watching with greater than usual interest. He laughed along with everyone else at first, but he had, also, long since stopped laughing. "LJ's manic behavior is worrisome," the doctor murmured and began taking notes. Moving closer to Ron, he whispered, "It's possible a long period of trauma, when suddenly over, can release a high level of adrenaline, similar to that of the fight-or-flight syndrome. That, mixed with the euphoria of finding he is not an orphan, being introduced to his

181

father, and suddenly removed from a terrifying situation could lead to a short-term mania, which would probably wear off. But as his… ahh… as *a* doctor, I want to follow up on LJ to be sure. That of course would be impossible, since Little Jimmy was hidden somewhere in the Witness Protection Program. Any way you can get me in touch with him?" Ron shrugged his shoulders.

The doctor put his pen and notepad in his jacket, and continued watching LJ. Then something Jimmy said caught his attention and he pulled out the pen and notepad and scribbled a few lines before taking out his cell phone and quickly leaving the library.

As the doctor left, Jimmy called out, "Quack! Quack! Quack!" and laughed hysterically though his eyes seamed fearful.

Little Jimmy droned on and on in between spurts of maniacal laughter, and the laugher that had earlier filled the library had been replaced with worried and uncomfortable silence. There was only one person in the room who was not worried about the teenager on the screen. But that was about to change.

"Now, let's see." LJ abruptly changed course. "Have we left anyone out. Any family ties *we missed*? Of course! What am I thinking? We cannot forget the Carloni family, can we? I mean, what would life be like without a good old-fashioned Italian vendetta. And speaking of Italian… How about the Amoretti family. Now there's some family ties worth delving into!"

Kat had pulled the plug on the video conference, saying, "Well it certainly looks like *someone* is enjoying his freedom! Can't blame the kid after all he's gone through." And then Catarina, who had anticipated an early end to the session, suggested another walk and fresh air and motioned to James to take the lead, along with another member of the staff to the kitchen.

Kat turned to say something to Ron, but just caught sight of his back as he left through the veranda door and headed towards the parking lot.

CHAPTER TEN

CONNECT THE CLUES TO
FOLLOW THE MONEY

BACK TO THE BEGINNING

Kat was still staring at Ron's brake lights disappearing down the driveway of Crossroads Inn Time B&B and Spa when her cell phone vibrated in her jacket.

The text from Ron simply said, "Don't share any more docs or journals! Don't trust anyone. BE CAREFUL AND STAY ALERT! Keep calm and distract The Insiders. I love you!"

Sudden dread filled Kat, as her eyes darted around watching The Insiders leaving the library, fighting the urge to run upstairs where her baby was napping.

A second text from Ron shook her phone, startling her. "I'm going to the beginning!"

"What?!" Kat stammered. "What does that mean…? Ooh. The beginning… " Kat nodded in agreement. That makes sense."

Movement made Kat look up from her phone.

Uncle Lenny was walking towards her. He was frowning. Kat froze.

Ron turned left on Highway 20 and fought the impulse to gun his Jeep, wishing he was in his squad car so he could speed. He also wished there were a faster way to get to Cobb Mountain. Ron remembered hearing that at one time the county had planned a bridge connecting Lucerne to Kelseyville, and wondered why it never came to fruition.

Scoffing at himself, Ron muttered, "Funny how your thoughts drift mindlessly trying to keep yourself calm when you're stressed." He hoped Kat's mind was doing the same. Ron knew it was a coin toss with Kat. At times she could be cool as a cucumber. But other times she… Ron said out loud. "Keep calm, Kat!" knowing she couldn't hear him.

Not knowing where Ron went or what to do, Kat decided that, since he instructed her not to share any more documents or journals, she would invent a new game.

Before her uncle could speak she said with a chuckle, "I have a new game for The Insiders…," trying to explain why she had been staring at her phone. But her attempted chuckle came out like a hen clucking after laying an egg. Then looking at her uncle as if she were taking him into her confidence she leaned forward and started explaining, "… since The Insiders are made up of friends and relatives who know me well enough to come to my memorial service," again trying humor. It fell flat on her uncle, who was still upset about being kept out of the loop. His frown deepened.

"Well, I'm thinking they all know about the troubles I've found myself in these past few years."

"Yeah," Lenny growled, "ever since you started hanging around with Ron!" Then remembering that she took on the investigation of the Lombardis on her own, and Ron enlisted his help to rescue Kat in the Mare Vista cellar. "And you decided to play Nancy Drew!" he added. Still no smile.

Relieved that Lenny didn't ask where Ron went, Kat quickly continued, "Well, all those cases were widely reported on in the press, so I think we'd be safe in discussing them openly without ruffling anyone's feathers, or interfering in the current investigations." Lenny just grunted, which Kat ignored.

"Money! As everyone knows 'money is the root of all evil,' and there is a *lot* of money from many sources involved in this case. Money being spent and even more money at stake! And *it all* seems to be related to…," Kat paused and chose her words carefully, "*yours* and Ron's past cases. So, I'm calling *our* new game: Connect the Clues to Follow the Money."

CONNECT THE CLUES TO FOLLOW THE MONEY

Kat added unnecessarily to Sgt. Lenard, "If we follow the money, it will lead us to who is behind all the minor games that lead to the major game—and the one key player who started the game and is pulling the…" Lenny's eyebrows pulled together as he glared.

"Kat, who are you trying to teach here? You think I need coaching? Or maybe you're trying to stall…"

Kat suddenly looked dramatically wide-eyed, cutting Lenny off, "Shh!" And motioning to the door, "Here they come!" she whispered.

James and another inn employee followed just behind The Insiders, and laid out an assortment

186

of snacks on the table. Lenny joined his wife, who had returned with the others. But to Kat, it seemed as if she entered from the opposite direction of the hall.

"Where has she been?" Kat worried, and despite knowing Little Ronnie was being watched over by *two* police women now, she quickly exited the library and ran upstairs to check on him.

After reassuring herself that her baby was safe, and confirming that *no one* had attempted to enter the nursery, Kat descended the grand stairway to the main hall. She wondered if her Auntie Antoinette had been eavesdropping on her conversation with Lenny. Nodding, she muttered, "The powder room is at the other end of the hall near the back door to the veranda." Then she thought, "Of course, she may have gone up to their bedroom… Still, I don't trust her. She is of the same bloodline as Francesca." Kat stopped abruptly, remembering Ron's text don't trust *anyone*. "And Angel!" she added with a shudder.

The Insiders took to the new game with even more enthusiasm than Kat had dared hope.

She let Lenny take the lead, and he started *at the beginning* with Heather Williams' body being discovered on Boggs' Mountain near a hiking trail.

While Lenny spoke, Kat studied the faces in the library, including her uncle's, as he led a lively interchange of clues and references. She couldn't see any suspicious expression. No one seemed to be hiding anything. But she knew someone was. Ron alluded to that in his text.

"What gets me," Angel mused, "is the boot prints."

187

"What do you mean?" Cassandra asked.

"The ones by the…" Angel's voice cracked. Clearing her throat, she went on, "By where they found Heather. They said it was made by a small foot inside a much larger boot."

"Oh, yeah. *That's right*. I remember that. Sgt. Lenard, what was *that* all about?" Cassandra asked. Kat made a mental note that her best friend from childhood didn't ask Jack Moran, the private investigator who Heather had hired to help her find her baby, and who helped Ron and Lenny on that and every subsequent case that followed… and most pertinent, Cassandra's fiancé, who was sitting right next to her!

Feeling Kat's penetrating eyes, Cassandra looked her way and quickly winked.

"Oh! She must see how I'm trying to get Uncle Lenny hooked into the game!" Kat smiled at her friend gratefully, but still wondered. Ron's words kept coming back to her.

"What are you talking about?" Mrs. Capra demanded.

Lenny got into his sergeant mode, "Well, let's see, our investigation uncovered a *so-called treatment* that the retreat on Cobb Mountain had been carrying out. All I know is that it was a ruse played out to scare… *to help* suicidal people realize they really didn't want to die. The ruse required a team of three. One to wait on the trail for the patient and stay just ahead of them as they went to a pre-agreed upon destination to do the deed, and to cause enough noise to get the person nervous. Then when they got to the rock formation where Miss Logan's body was found, they would allow the patient to get a couple glimpses of them… wearing a long trench coat, darting behind the trees. The theory was that it would scare them and send them running back to their car. The masked person would follow them to keep them running, and to make sure they made it safely to their car."

"I thought you said there was a team of three," quizzed Caroline.

"Yes, well there were two others dressed the same and wearing a similar mask waiting in the wings. One would cover the only other path back to the parking lot. And the third person would be waiting near the rock formation to approach the patient face-on to trigger the desired results, if they hadn't already been scared back to the car." Lenny's disgust with this ruse was obvious.

"What about the boot prints? What was that all about?" Angel got back to her original question.

"Well, there could be a number of reasons. It could be as simple as the clinic only having large sized boots…"

"No!" Angel sighed, "I mean why was it a big deal? I mean…" Angel stammered and her face reddened a bit. "The newspaper made it seem like it was a major part of the investigation… and it had worked dozens of times before. But something went wrong with Heather..." Angel's voice trailed off evoking an outpouring of sideways glances. Some sympathetic. Some not so much.

The Insiders must have remembered how Angel's Aunt Antoinette had disclosed the fact that Angel had been a patient at the retreat, and had volunteered there. Perhaps some were now wondering if she had also participated in the ruse.

Lenny coughed and started up again, "Well,

it was important because it proved someone was there standing toe-to-toe with Heather moments before she… before the gun was fired.”

“But I do think it’s important that there was a small foot in the boot,” Theo muttered almost to herself. When she realized others had heard she added, “Perhaps someone was trying to disguise their footprints to make it seem it was a much larger person that confronted Heather…”

“That’s ridiculous! Why would someone *do that*?” Angel asked a bit too loudly.

“No, Theo could be on to something.” Catarina spoke out in her sister’s defense. “Maybe someone wanted Heather dead. Maybe they took advantage of the situation to make sure Heather shot herself.”

“Or perhaps used the gun themselves.” Eduardo speculated.

“Only the three-person team from the retreat knew Heather was planning a suicide that night.” Lenny butted in gruffly, clearly taking offence to his investigation being second-guessed. “Not to mention, two of them had large feet.”

“And the other masked person was close enough to see Heather being confronted, and she willingly submitted to a polygraph…” Lenny stopped midsentence.

Realizing his former boss had just revealed the fact that a female was on the team that night, Jack, who up to this point had remained quiet, abruptly added, “Everyone from the retreat was questioned thoroughly and *no one* knew Heather had a gun.”

“Someone else could have known. Someone

who had experienced the ruse firsthand. They would know the route Heather would have walked and her destination. They could have beat the team there and hid until the right moment and did *or said* something to Heather that pushed her over the edge," Theo insisted.

"That would match up with the testimony of the team members," Lenny conceded. "The two watching the lower paths said, hearing the gunshot, they ran towards the rocks and almost bumped into each other where the paths joined and raced as they continued towards the rocks where they saw the… saw Heather lying on the ground. And their other *'team member'* was standing up the steep part of the hill. She could never have made it back up there in that short of time," Lenny said. "And she claimed to have seen some type of interchange with the clown-faced person who was face-to-face with Heather. And in the brief light made by the gunshot, she saw a smile on Heather's face. A *sick smile*."

"That would mean it was premeditated," Jack stated matter-of-factly.

"And murder!" Lenny added grimly looking squarely at his one-time protégée, who nodded back.

The library went quiet to the point of getting uncomfortable.

Kat broke the silence with, "So, what do we know about Heather Williams… I mean Logan? Her background?"

"*You* tell us, Kat!" Cassandra chided. "You're the super sleuth here." Her remark made Lenny and Jack grumble, and caused a much-needed laugh from The Insiders.

After the laughter subsided, Kat took a breath

and began, "Well, Heather's father, William Logan, had inherited wealth, and was a successful business owner in his own right. He and his wife died in what was at first deemed an accident, leaving Heather's aunt as trustee. When she died of what was also an assumed accident, her husband, Heather's uncle, Ralph Henderson, took over as trustee.

"Heather was to inherit big time! Soon after Henderson took charge of her, she had a baby out of wedlock. Before she realized she was pregnant, her new boyfriend had suddenly been called to active duty, and was shipped to a warzone where he almost immediately was wounded and went missing in action. Heather's newborn son was now heir to a fortune of unimaginable size.

"However, Henderson bribed personnel at the clinic where Heather gave birth to lie about the baby dying and conspired with them to cover up an illegal adoption.

"Heather knew her baby had been born healthy and suspected her uncle of foul play and, out of fear for her own safety and the hope of finding her child, she ran away from the clinic. She took what money she had access to, which was quite a bit, to create a new identity and disappeared to Lake County."

"Hey! What did you mean, her close relative's deaths were first *thought* accidents?" Angel demanded.

"Yeah! What's the story there?" John Buchanan wanted to know. Or maybe he was just backing up Angel's question. Kat was unsure.

"Well, yes. There's a postscript to that story," Lenny took the floor again. "Although the death of

Heather Logan's parents and aunt were at first declared accidents, new evidence surfaced and the cases were reopened, and Ralph Henderson was tried and convicted of their murders. We added the charges of kidnapping and child endangerment leading to death, for which he was also tried and convicted, which added years to his sentence."

"And we all thought that would be the end of his story. But… well, it didn't turn out that way." Kat said glumly.

"What?!" The Insiders yelled out almost simultaneously! "He got away with murder and child stealing?"

"How?!" the frail little Mrs. Capra turned into a grizzly bear!

Lenny, looking at Kat, replied, "Well, that's a long story. And like Kat said, we need to follow the clues to *the money* to get all the answers. And few have brought more money into this county than *the Lombardi family*.

"Now that's a hair-raising story that got Kat run off the road and later almost ran over, and then chased through an empty mansion in the middle of nowhere, and trapped by rats in the basement and almost killed! That was before she *married* Ron, but if he hadn't been following her, no telling what would've…"

Again, in unison The Insiders yelled, "What?! He was following her?!"

"I know, I know. That sounds like he was stalking her, but take my word as her uncle, *someone needed to!!* She wouldn't listen to my advice and stay clear of the matter." Lenny's face turned red with anger sharing how Kat had defied him while trying

193

to prove the elderly Mrs. Lombardi was missing and in danger.

"So anyway," Lenny continued, "that case is how most of us became acquainted with Guido and Francesca Lombardi, but the Lombardi family had traveled to Lake County by wagon train and settled up on Cobb, in the 1800's."

"So was the old woman found?" John Buchanan asked.

"In a way, yes. She had died, and was replaced by her cousin, who took her identity. The way Guido explained it, it seemed like they were up against the wall and it all made sense. The perps chasing Kat were arrested, and the whole thing was smoothed over and forgotten. But after The Game the other night, and Guido and Francesca's arrest, I'm not so certain.

"But we're not to speak of that." Jack said quickly. Lenny growled, clearly not happy at being silenced by an underling.

"Well, Sgt. Lenny, I have another question for you!" Mrs. Capra called out, still visibly upset. "Just who was the inside person Henderson had in the foster system? I bet a dime-to-a-dollar it was the same no-good woman who landed Little Jimmy in that foster home of Melbourne's, or whatever his real name was!"

"Yes, you are so right!" Jack blurted. "You are quite a smart cookie to figure that out!"

Mrs. Capra just frowned, "I'm old, but I'm not *dumb*!" Then turning back to Lenny, she took an even sterner tone, "Well, cut to the chase! What's the scoop there? Was that old bag Jones connected to both Henderson and Melbourne?"

Lenny struggled to hold back a chuckle at hearing the little old lady use such strong terms. "Yes, she was put into position by Henderson, but her greed took over and when she told her crooked husband and greedy brother there was a fortune to be found, they took it from there."

"Well, I was sure glad to hear they all went to prison! After all they put my Little Jimmy and the other boys through, I hope they threw away the key!" Seeing Lenny's face, she questioned, "They *are* still in jail, aren't they?"

While Lenny searched for the right words, Mrs. Capra straightened up in her chair and shouted, "That's how my Little Jimmy ended up in the so-called '*care*' of Guido and Francesca in the first place! So you better tell me right now. Are Melbourne and Mr. and Mrs. Jones still in jail?"

Fearing Mrs. Capra would become so upset that she'd have another stroke or heart attack, Lenny looked to his niece for help.

"Mrs. Capra, we are all upset, but I know you love Little Jimmy more than all of us combined. And I know you are feeling guilty that it was your ill health that led to him being taken out of your care. I know that, because Ron and I also feel guilty at dragging our feet, and then we both got sick and couldn't take him into our home. We all feel we let Little Jimmy down when he needed us the most. But what we have to remember is how much we did help him before that, and how much we helped him after and continue to help him. I don't think there was ever a child loved by so many." By the time Kat had finished speaking, she was kneeling at Mrs. Capra's feet, looking into her eyes, and holding both her

195

hands in her own. Both women had tears running down their faces. As did most of the women *and* men in the library. But not all.

After a few moments, Lenny, trying to sound calm, said "Okay, before we go any further, how about a break? I know I could use one," he mumbled as he strode quickly out the door and down the hall to the men's room. The Insiders burst into laughter, including Mrs. Capra.

After the short break and all were seated back in the library, and while Lenny, Jack and Kat were deciding who would take the floor first to speak, Theo stood up and walked to the front. Looking at the group seated in the room and those who had taken the lead in all the cases that had been discussed, she quietly said, "I know my soon-to-be ex-husband was involved in some of your cases. Maybe all of them.

"For sure, the one that began with this inn, Crossroads and the *one we can't talk about*.

"But I have reason to believe he is involved with more. I'm seeing a pattern of how all these cases are intertwined. For example, The Lombardi family is a name I'm quite familiar with. My ex has been working for that family since I met him, as well as the other big 'family' name from Los Gatos. I was married to him for a very long time, and although I never knew he worked for the mob, I did know he wasn't a good man. I knew he was dishonest, and greedy. Over the years I've heard him mention many of the names I heard the other night at The Game, including Myers and Logan. And for the record, he had his sights set on a mansion in the Santa Cruz Mountains called *Mare Vista* that the Lombardis own. But what really made him drool was the fortune on Mount Hannah which is owned by the Logans. By now we must all know Little Jimmy is the rightful heir to all that. So, if we're connecting the clues to find the money, I think we've found it. So now let's follow it to the main guy. My ex… Steven Pinero has my vote."

The silence could be cut with a knife.

Kat wished ever so much that Ron would return. Although she had already come to the same conclusion about everything and everyone being connected, now that it had been voiced out in the open for all to hear, before Kat had figured out who among The Insiders was not to be trusted, and who was pulling the strings, Kat had every reason to be afraid. As she was thinking it, her aunt voiced it.

"So, what we need now is to find out who the puppeteer is who has been pulling all the strings of those good-for-nothing varmints, before their attorneys cut a deal and they get their walking papers and are set free to continue with their evil *murder* plans." Antoinette's cold words filled Kat's veins with ice.

CHAPTER ELEVEN

PUPPETEER OR PUPPET?

WHO'S PULLING THE STRINGS?

Antoinette's words still hung in the air, and the library was stone quiet. Jack finally broke the silence by standing up and taking Cassandra's hand. He led everyone on a walk around the lower garden paths.

Lenny started out the door to join The Insiders on their walk, but seemed to change his mind and turned facing Kat, standing between her and the door.

"So just who is behind all this?" Kat stammered nervously, her eyes searching for an escape. "I mean who originated the scheme? The game?"

"The game?"

Lenny asked. "Yes! The game. The *real* game! Who manipulated all these people into… into whatever," Kat continued to ramble, as she walked to position herself with the large library table between Lenny and herself, "I don't even know what's going on. Or why! Seems everyone… They all had goals… *all evil*. But different levels of evil. But evil nonetheless. And yet they're *all connected*.

Lenny moved closer to the table and as Kat spoke, she slid down the edge of the table maneuvering herself closer and closer to the door, while Lenny stayed directly across from her on his side of the table, "But I think…" Kat hesitated, "No! *I know* there's someone who has a bigger goal than all of them combined. And more evil." Though Kat tried to portray a nonchalant attitude, her eyes couldn't hide her fear. "And that *someone* has manipulated them all to assembling here in Lake County, where he *or she* could play their own games on each of them while getting them to help him *or her* achieve whatever goal it is that motivates him… or her… Does that make sense?" Kat's voice wavered.

"I don't know, Kat," her uncle stated dryly. "Can someone actually do that?"

"I don't know. All I know is there is one person behind everything. I don't know who. Or why. But I've got to find out before…" Kat's desperate eyes looked up towards the ceiling. Her baby was sleeping upstairs, unaware that a plot to end his life had been in place even before he was born. "I have to find who's behind all this *before…*"

An overwhelming feeling of helplessness swept over her.

Suddenly Ron, who had been standing in the doorway, quickly rushed to her side and took her in his arms. "Kat we've got this! We're almost there. Together we'll figure it out!" He hugged her tighter and was happy she couldn't see the fear in his eyes.

"Oh, Ron I'm so glad you're back! I was so worried! And afraid because I didn't know who you meant for me to…"

Ron turned quickly to look at Lenny. "So, everything go alright?"

"Yeah, just like I said in my text! Thanks for texting me back. That was a great idea you and Kat had." Lenny said grinning.

"Yep, Ron, we've been rehashing old cases we've had over the years, and you were right. There was more information to be learned. And some either withheld information when going on your 'ride-alongs,' or they had temporary amnesia, because they've been doing a lot of talking and remembering!"

Looking out the window, Ron nodded at The Insiders who were headed back up towards the veranda. He said quietly, "Lenny, by now you probably need a break from The Insiders. And I'm *sure not* ready to interact with them yet," Ron laughed. "Seriously, I think I should lay low for a bit. They seem to talk more freely when I'm not around. I'm sure Kat and Jack can handle them for a while longer. How about you and I hide out in the pantry," Ron laughed again, "and bring me up to date."

Lenny slapped Ron on the back, and laughed heartily, "Sure thing *Buddy*," making reference to the nickname Kat had for him in their early years of dating.

More relief washed over Kat, making it necessary for her to sit down. Not only did Ron return safely from wherever he rushed off to, but her dear Uncle Lenny was obviously not one of the ones Ron told her not to trust!

"You go ahead, I better duck out the side door," Ron said to Lenny, "and I'll come in the back door after everyone's inside." Ron gave Kat a look that made her worries return, and brought her to her feet.

Ron hugged Kat and whispered in her ear. "Lots to say. But later. You're doing a great job. Just stay calm and let them talk. Let them *all* talk. And when the time is right, go upstairs and stay with Ronnie."

Wide-eyed, Kat whispered, "but how will I know when…"

"You'll know!" Ron said as he slipped out the door.

"What can I say to get them talking again," Kat murmured to herself. She needn't have worried.

"So just who organized this Italian grudge match?" Cassandra was asking as the group entered the library.

"*Vendetta!* It's called a vendetta. An Italian grudge is a vendetta!" Angel corrected her sister's best friend. "And vendettas are no joking matter! They're taken seriously by those involved. It's a vow to right a wrong… or to vindicate someone's virtue. And those making the vow would be willing to carry it out to the death. Theirs or *others*!"

"Angel Amoretti!" Caroline turned and with hands on her hips, scolded her youngest daughter, "You've been listening to your sister too much! There's been quite enough of this Italian talk for one family!"

Making the Italian hand gesture with thumb touching fingers, "What do you mean? Italian blood flows through my veins just as much as Kat's!" Angel teased her mother using an Italian accent. Caroline just walked away shaking her head.

Laughing before jumping in to continue their conversation, Kat turned to Cassandra and asked, "Who do you think? Any ideas?"

"What?" Angel looked confused.

Cassandra said, "If you'd be serious for a minute, I asked who started the vendetta?"

"Oh, yeah. Well, I don't know." Turning to Caroline, Angel said, "Mom? Earlier you were saying you thought it was probably…. Who was it?"

"Oh, well I only suggested that *maybe* it was Contessa. Kat? What do you think? Did Contessa enlist her family to swear a vow to carry out revenge for all the trouble and pain she had to endure in America? That makes sense to me."

"No, I doubt it." Kat replied thoughtfully, "Contessa was basically good. Just think how long and hard she tried to honor Caroline O'Shay's dying wish. Even long after Celina McKenzie went missing, she did her best to see that Sam Spears got the documents, even though she could've sold them for a lot of money."

"Maybe it was her sons," Tessie joined the debate. "No wait! Never mind. I remember now, one was good like his mother. Too good to do harm to anyone. And though the other was rotten to the core, he would never go on a noble quest to even the score for anyone. Not even his mother. He was too self-centered, like the men before him."

"Well… there's Maria?" Sal offered, "Or Sophia? Or maybe both. They both knew their grandmother's story. And they both came to America." Sal looked around to see if anyone agreed with him. "What do you think?" he asked, hands out with palms up. "Possible?"

"Possible, but not probable," Catarina argued. Neither of them is alive now. And someone is still carrying out this Italian thing!"

"No… Maria and Sophia are *not* alive, but someone very close to them is. *Francesca*!" Kat said lifting an eyebrow.

"Yes!" Cindy suddenly cried out. "I'm glad someone brought her name up! I've never trusted Francesca. She always seemed too sweet and mousey. And yet she's always in the middle of every conversation, and in group she seems to know too much about everyone." Cindy looked like she wished she could take her words back. As an employee of the retreat, she signed a confidentiality agreement. "She had Contessa's letters and her journal… so she knows all of it." Cindy practically whispered.

Angel ignored Cindy's breach and blurted out, "Yeah, but is she evil enough… and sick enough? Maybe."

"Or greedy enough?" Catarina added wryly.

"I don't know about all that, but only Francesca is *alive now*. She is Contessa's only blood relative. Around here anyway." Kat stated, before murmuring, "That we know of."

All eyes turned to Kat.

Angel walked over and stood in front of her sister, and looking into her eyes demanded, "Are you holding back information?"

"No. I was just wondering if we've spent enough time going over bloodlines?" Kat asked while silently congratulating herself for opening up another avenue of thought to discuss, and keep The Insiders' minds occupied and interested.

"Bloodlines?" Lenny asked.

"Yes! Bloodlines." Sal agreed with Kat almost too loudly. "We need to know who we're looking for. We need to know if Contessa's sons have offspring that may be… may be right in this very room!" The wide-eyed Insiders glanced around the room searching faces, as if they would recognize

203

a relative of Contessa's.

While they searched faces, Kat watched for any nervous twitches or behavior.

Sal looked at her and said, "Kat you've charted out bloodlines, right? Don't you have them upstairs?"

"Was that it. Was that my que to go upstairs to Baby Ronnie's room?" Kat wondered. Regardless, she was way past ready for a break.

As Kat ascended the stairs, the murmuring from the library floated up behind her, getting more quiet with each step.

Kat tapped on the door and it was opened by one of the police officers that Bill Norris sent.

Kat went over to her baby and picking him up, she sat down in the rocker and closed her eyes and buried her face in her baby's blankets, breathing deeply as if memorizing her baby's smell. Ronnie slept while Kat was having a silent meltdown.

What next? She felt safer upstairs behind a locked door with two armed guards, but people she loved were still on the floor beneath her. Her mother, her sister, Cassandra… Kat paused. Normally her aunt and uncle would be right up there next to her mother and sister. But now she wasn't sure. All she knew is that the thought of leaving the safety of this room made her ill.

Kat pulled out her cell and texted Ron, "What now?" His immediate reply was "Stay put!" Not knowing what else to do, Kat continued to rock Ronnie.

"Glad you could join us," Lenny said gruffly as Doctor Fleming entered the library. The doctor replied pleasantly, "Yes, I'm glad as well. Good to get away from the retreat and my clinic. It's been busy. So, what have I missed?"

"Not much," Ron said as he strolled into the library with a stack of printed bloodline forms, which he scattered on the nearby coffee table. "Kat is with the baby, but she sent these down. She said you all wanted to take a look."

The Insiders enthusiastically pored over the papers. Sal stepped up and began spreading out the forms on the floor so everyone could pick up a family tree.

"This doesn't seem right...," Antoinette started to say, but seemed to change her mind. No one noticed... except Ron. And the doctor.

A lively discussion ensued with some laughter, but quickly got serious. Soon the papers were laid down and Sal gathered them up.

Finally, Angel spoke up. "So, LJ is in all the uplines from Spears, O'Shay, Myers, and Logan. All of them! What does that mean?"

"It means he's a bloody millionaire!" Sal grunted.

"Billionaire." Jack corrected him.

"And he's related to..." Sal stopped short.

"Yes. Everyone." Jack said flatly.

"Wait, let me get this straight." Angel said, "So Little Jimmy's mother, Heather Williams—whose real last name was Logan, and Little Jimmy's dad is the great, great grandchild of the mean Old Man Myers' daughter, and she married Logan's son."

"That's right. Related to Myers, too," Jack said. "Logan and Myers. Like I said, everyone."

"And us. LJ is related to us, too." Angel said, happily.

"And how is that, again?" Cassandra asked, clearly confused.

"*The point this is*," John Buchanan stated bluntly, "LJ is related to everyone, and everything is connected to him. Oh, and everyone wants him dead."

"That's pretty calloused, John!" frowned Angel.

"I'm sorry, Angel." John scrunched his body down lower in the chair he was sitting in.

"Okay, so someone said LJ's dad has been living here in Lake County. Do we know him? Has anyone met him?" Tessie wondered.

"Kat has!" everyone said in unison. Looking around, Antoinette asked, "Where's Kat?"

"Upstairs with the baby." Ron said almost coldly. Lenny looked up sharply.

"Not face-to-face." Angel said.

"What?" Caroline asked.

"Kat has never met LJ's dad face-to-face. Only on Internet chats. And he always used an avatar. He said it was because he was scarred from the war."

"How is it no one's noticed him then? A scarred-up person walking around isn't exactly invisible," John Buchanan said, giving Angel a sideways glance to make sure she wasn't offended.

"Well, actually you all have probably… if not met him, been in the same room with him at one time or another. He's taken menial jobs around the county as a janitor, waiter, or window washer. Anything where he could be invisible while eavesdropping or get access to a little computer time." Jack said nonchalantly, winking at Ron who chuckled.

Everyone looked up as Bill Norris walked in the room. He wasn't chuckling. And the grin was quickly gone from Ron's face.

Bill looked at Lenny who walked swiftly up to greet him. "Good to see you again, Bill." Lenny said.

"Not social this time, I'm afraid, Len," Bill said. "Get your wife and quietly join me in the parlor." And Bill left the room. Ron's face was ashen as his wife's aunt and uncle walked out of the library. His eyes met with Jack's and they both looked away.

Jack walked swiftly to the front of the room "Can I have everyone's attention, please?

"I think we've played 'Family Tree' long enough. But it was fun, wasn't it?

"But I understand Sal and Eduardo are serving up some dyn-o-mite BBQ ribs down by the pool." Jack grinned, and motioned everyone to follow him.

Ron looked at Dr. Fleming, who nodded and said, "I'll wait here for you."

Ron walked into the hallway and towards the stairs, and heaved a deep sigh before taking the stairs two at a time.

As the couple walked down the stairs, Kat said, "I'm so glad to finally be able to talk to you, Ron. While you were gone, I started thinking…" Kat stopped on the landing and faced Ron.

"Ron, think back to each case you've had since you became a deputy, each mystery. All the good guys… all the bad guys. Ask yourself, "was justice really served? Were the ones you put behind bars really behind each of the cases? Or was there someone else we overlooked? Or didn't uncover?"

Not waiting for an answer, Kat continued, "In all of your past cases. Everything you've been involved with, Ron. I think there was *one person*—the same person who was calling all the shots in each case. Manipulating everyone into thinking *they* were in charge but that one person was the one pulling their strings. Like a puppet and puppeteer."

Ron had begun walking slowly down the stairs with Kat's arm in his hand.

"Did you hear me, Ron?" Kat frowned, "One person all this time behind each one of your cases. One!

"Ron, I've spent all afternoon going over the list of possibilities, and eliminated most of the suspicious characters. But I still have a list that consists of only those who would know what went on up in the Cobb Mountain Retreat. Particularly on the Bogg's Hiking Trails.

"Any one of them could have known and been there ahead of the others, disguised as they were in long trench coat and Halloween mask. And as evidence indicated, the person standing there looking eye-to-eye through a mask with Heather that fateful night was wearing large ill-fitted shoes.

"So, whose eyes were Heather looking at as she peered through the eye holes? She was startled… terrified… looking for a place to run… looking for safety. The doctor's theory—acted out so many times with success—but with one failure. When those who witnessed what happened that night finally started talking to each other they all reported that everything went as usual. She was stalked. Startled. Hid. And then confronted by the terrifying mask-wearing participant in the plan. Everything went according to plan until… they all said Heather seemed to notice something about the eyes through the mask that night. Familiar eyes? Who was it?

"Cindy's? She would certainly recognize her roommate's eyes, but would that have created the ill results? No. But I found out that she was on the schedule to assist in the plan that night. The shoes would no doubt have been too large for her tiny feet. But she had been one of the first sightings on the path, and had to remain at the top of the path where she could keep her position, to keep her eyes on Heather as she encountered the mask-wearing person before running back to her car. She only left the position when the gun went off to duck behind a tree. She said when she peeked out, the doctor and John were standing over the body. I believe her.

"So okay, perhaps it was Jack's eyes Heather saw through the eyes of the mask. She'd seen him many times at the retreat, even in their cabin since he was Cindy's cousin. And since Heather was his client, she could very well have confided in him as to her plans. And since his cousin Cindy had recently gone for a hike herself, carrying a water bottle, Jack would know where to be. What to wear. Was his loyalty bought off by someone who would profit greatly by Heather's suicide?

"Who had money and would profit by that happening? How about John Buchanan? His father had coerced him to enter the program at the retreat in the first place. Could this have been the goal to that course?

"And then, as much as I hate to think of her that way, there's Angel. No, Angel had a rock-solid alibi that night. Not that she'd need one. She had absolutely no motive.

"How about the doctor? He and John both said they saw each other as they were both running towards Heather. Where exactly did they see each other? Could one of them have just turned around so it appeared as though he was running towards the scream, when in fact, he had just been running away from the body? John's feet were large. Too large that even the boot that made the oversized shoeprints would've been snug. So if it wasn't Cindy, Jack, Angel, John… the last man standing is—Dr. Richard Fleming. He's also the only one who seems not to have been affected one way or another in all this. He's come out unscathed… as a matter of fact, he seems to have prospered. I'm referring to his addition and plans for a new treatment center.

"So that's it, Ron. I think it was the doctor that night with Heather! What do you think?" Kat didn't give her husband a chance to answer before she continued on toward the library.

Reaching the library door, Kat paused before adding, "The thing I don't know, Ron, is *who*. Who was calling the shots? Who is the puppeteer? Who do you think it could be? Is it a bad guy disguising himself, like Steven Pinero? Or my Auntie Antoinette, who hid knowledge of the vendetta all these decades? Or maybe Contessa? I know she's hiding something. But maybe Dr. Fleming is also the puppeteer, besides being the last one to see into Heather's eyes. Yes! I think it's him. He's been involved with each case you've… Dr Fleming's the last man standing. He's our guy. He's the puppeteer! I think…Oh!"

Surprised to see Dr. Fleming as they walked into the library, Kat stopped mid-sentence. "Everyone gone for another walk?," she asked with a forced laugh.

Dr. Fleming just smiled, "Hello, Kat."

Ron turned to his wife and said, "We've got something to tell you, Kat. But first… remember when I told you that Dr. Fleming said he had a story but he wouldn't tell us yet?

"Yes," Kat said slowly.

"Well, he's ready to tell us," Ron looked at the doctor.

DR FLEMING's STORY

The doctor, without any hesitation, began speaking. "Fleming is not my real last name. It was changed when I resigned from the military, where I had led treatment for Post Traumatic Stress Syndrome in military personnel before being assigned to a top-secret division where I helped train handpicked soldiers for special ops.

"That's where I came across Jimmy's dad, who had the highest IQ of anyone the Army had filtered into this Special Operations unit. He was called The Watcher. He could turn any computer into a tool to find and track anyone who ever signed on to a computer. Then he would 'watch' them. He'd manipulate them. He opened doors his subjects didn't even know they were trying to get through. He'd help them 'find' the people, places, events… before they themselves knew they were looking for

211

them. Almost as if he were reading their minds.

"But he wasn't reading their minds. He was *putting the thoughts into their mind*s with a touch of a key. Then he'd watch them and manipulate them. That's how he got the name, The Watcher. Or maybe he gave himself the name, I don't know. But I had never come across anyone as brilliant as The Watcher. He was fascinating to be around. He could 'watch' a dozen people simultaneously, moving them around in their lives as if they were pawns on a chessboard. The Army had big plans for The Watcher. The only problem was The Watcher was on to their game, and he manipulated instructors into doing what ever, and taking him to where ever, he wanted. They didn't even realize they were the ones being trained. But I knew. And I was fascinated. And The Watcher knew I knew. And he was fascinated. It was during the final part of his training when someone with a higher pay grade than I snatched him up and sent him to the front line.

"The Watcher was shot in the back by *friendly fire*, left in the desert and captured, tortured… and escaped.

"Knowing he'd been set up, The Watcher didn't reattach himself to his unit, or any other, for that matter. Instead, he found his way onto a junket traveling to Mexico. On board he found access to a computer, and pulling up his military records, he traced his transfer and change of military status back to a Los Gatos attorney who represented the Annunzio Real Estate Firm. None other than *Stephen Pinero*. He hacked Pinero's info and found that the real estate company had a habit of acquiring estates and conglomerates. And they had their sights on the

212

Logan Corporation. The Watcher realized it was in the firm's *best interest* that there be no more Logan heirs produced. Hence his sudden reclassification and deployment, which left Heather Logan alone and under the control of her uncle, Ralph Henderson.

"Pinero also had professional and personal interests in Lake County. As you know, he had his claws dug deeply into and ready to pounce on Crossroads Inn Time Bed & Breakfast and Spa several years ago, for which he fled the country to avoid punishment by the Los Gatos Annunzio Real Estate Firm. Besides Crossroads Inn, Pinero had become a silent campaign manager for the Lake County high sheriff and was directing his career towards Congress, and knocking anything and everyone out of the way. That is, until recently… which we're not supposed to be speaking of.

"And besides, I digress." The doctor smiled a bit. "Getting back to The Watcher, by the time he walked down the gangplank in Ensenada, he had a passport and other papers needed to board a cruise ship and headed to San Francisco disguised as a waiter."

"So, that's how you're connected to Little Jimmy! I always wondered. I thought perhaps he had been treated at your clinic," Kat smiled.

"Well… that I can't speak of… patient privilege, etc. But yes, I first came to know of Little Jimmy through his dad, whom I had tested personally and his IQ was higher than any recorded in history. I would need his permission to reveal it. I've also tested his son. But I'm sure you already know how brilliant LJ is. Getting back to The Watcher… he told me he wanted to use his gift to benefit society, and

213

refused to be used by any government or military. The Watcher didn't... doesn't... like institutions or traditional educational platforms, which only served to put limits on what he could study and just slowed him down.

"Sadly, the government and military had different plans for him and he found himself trapped, so to speak. So, he took a hike. Literally. He hiked up Mount Hamilton and camped, living off the land while... umm... he found a weak spot in the security system in the planetarium up there. So, he spent his nights hacking their computers.

"The Watcher thought he'd broken free, and he could have been. If he hadn't met and fallen in love with the incredible Heather Logan. Or maybe he manipulated the meeting. Just like he manipulated LJ to spend more time on the mountain and away from the Lombardis. I'm not sure. But Heather loved all the same things The Watcher loved, like hiking up on Mount Hamilton, where they met. They started hiking the other mountains that surrounded Santa Clara Valley. It was the happiest The Watcher had ever been.

"It went ok for a while, but somehow her uncle caught wind of their relationship and he restricted her to her home.

"The Watcher hacked her computer and started teaching her how to not only hack computers, but also how to get a new identity. They were planning on leaving the area together, and he would help her get control of her trust fund and inheritance. But before they could put their plan into action, the uncle found out.

"That's also when the military tracked The

214

Watcher down and someone pulled strings to send LJ's brilliant father to the front line. The official report said he was uncooperative with the powers that be, but I knew the real reason.

"Through my counseling sessions with high-level military personnel, I had quite the dossier built up—but couldn't ethically, or safely, inform on them.

"So, I resigned from the military and took some time for myself, trying to convince myself that The Watcher could take care of himself. I was right. And not only himself, but me as well.

"One morning when I logged onto my computer, I found that he'd hacked my computer to tell me that he left the military and was traveling across the ocean and would be in touch, but added that I should know that that he'd changed my name, identity and history. The Watcher built a new professional history and got me hired at a San Jose hospital where he knew Heather had been admitted for depression, by her uncle who was her guardian— and large hospital donor— paid for out of Heather's trust fund. While there, it was also discovered that she was pregnant. She was kept in the hospital for the remainder of the pregnancy. But I was able to control her treatment. I never mentioned that I knew The Watcher, but I did what was best for the girl to ensure she and her baby would be healthy. The baby was in fact born healthy. I witnessed the birth and examined him myself.

"But there was a quick adoption, and Heather was told he had been stillborn. She knew it was a lie. I had access to his medical and adoption records and slipped a copy into her robe pocket so only she would see it. She slipped out of the hospital and disappeared.

"Shortly after that, I woke up and found that a grant had been written in my name, which included enough money to start my clinic and retreat.

"The Watcher had chosen Lake County to be my new home. He had followed the baby's trail, though difficult due to the extreme measures taken to leave no paper trail. The Watcher also 'helped' Heather to follow the trail, by hacking into her computer and creating hints when she would search certain words. But it was difficult to keep up with her movements, because she only used library computers and kept changing library branches and even towns so the IPs would change. He regretted having taught her that. But gradually The Watcher was able to direct Heather to Lake County where he knew their son was living. But she suddenly stopped using computers. She realized she was being traced and was afraid it was her uncle, since she had written the state department and had received notice that The Watcher had been wounded and was missing and presumed dead.

"Heather was heartbroken, but she didn't give up on finding her son. She hired a private investigator who referred her to a family lawyer who just looked on the surface and said her baby died shortly after the adoption. That was more than she could take, and she sunk into a deep depression.

"The Watcher relocated to Lake County but stayed under the radar. He continued to help me— from inside my computer. He expedited the setting up of the clinic and retreat. Then he 'arranged' an accidental meeting with Heather, who accepted my

216

invitation to attend a seminar at the retreat on Cobb Mountain. She soon was staying at the retreat and attending all classes and groups.

"The Watcher had begun leaving bread crumbs on the PIs computer to lead Jack, Heather's PI, to Little Jimmy. Just a little at a time, for two reasons. First, because The Watcher feared if Heather found LJ before his plan came to fruition, they would both be murdered. And secondly, to give me more time to prepare her for his reappearance. He was very worried that she hated him for abandoning her.

"But of course, the one thing The Watcher didn't know was that she had hired an attorney. And that the attorney gave her the report of the adopted baby's death and that's what sent her prematurely into the woods on her death march.

"I had hoped she would not 'take that walk into the woods as soon as she did. She wasn't ready. But, even so, I was sure she would be helped, just as dozens had been by then.

"When The Watcher realized Heather's plan, he rushed to the retreat, grabbed a trench coat, mask, and the first boots he could find. The boots were so big, they dwarfed his feet inside making the footprint that opened up this case.

"He hoped beyond hope that if he could get close enough to look her in the eye, she would recognize his eyes.

"That was the problem. Had it not been his eyes she saw, *she may have* run back to her car. She would join the long list of the retreat's successes. *But it was his eyes.* She recognized his eyes and all fear left her. As always, his warm eyes calmed her. She was calm. She had always said he helped her be calm. That smile wasn't one of revenge. It wasn't cynical, as Cindy had thought. It was relief. She was relieved to see that her one true love had survived the war. Heather was happy to see him. But she couldn't... she just couldn't bring herself to tell him he had been a father. And she felt she let them both down. The baby and The Watcher. If only she'd left when he asked her to, everything would be different. But she was afraid. She allowed her uncle to get control of her again. Heather couldn't bring herself to tell him he *had* been a father, but was a father no more. So, she smiled, and told him good bye."

After a very long silence, Kat whispered, "So, who was pulling the strings? I think you know, don't you?"

The doctor sat in silence, and Kat whispered again, "Is it my aunt? Antoinette?"

Finally, the doctor spoke. He revealed that the day Kat pulled into the back lot of the retreat, he had been waiting for her. It was all set up for her to meet LJ's dad. It was he who chased her there. To the safety of the retreat. LJ was also at the retreat, having come in a back entrance, and it was he who was on the other end of the open conference phone.

He was waiting for the all clear from Fleming and the three of them were going to talk to Kat: LJ, Fleming, and LJ's father. However, someone threw a hammer in their plan. That person showed up unannounced and somehow seemed to know that something was about to happen and insisted she was in crisis and was waiting in a room next to the office

218

where she could hear every pin drop. That person was... the person who has manipulated each and every person who were participants of The Game. That person was even able to pull the wool over the eyes of the Los Gatos Mob. That person was able to enlist Antoinette to join in the very vendetta she had resisted her entire life. That person was... *Francesca Carloni Lombardi.*"

Last man standing may have been Dr. Richard Fleming. But *the woman* was ready to take it all.

As Kat and Ron were absorbing all of what the doctor had revealed, Bill Norris walked in with Lenny and Antoinette. Antoinette's eyes were red from crying. She walked over and sat next to her niece, and put her arm around her.

"Are you okay, Auntie?" Kat worried.

"I'm okay... *now.*" Antoinette replied. "Yesterday, I asked Ron to call his stepdad for me, and I've told him all I've been holding on to. My entire life, I've kept secrets. Family secrets. But no more. Bill knows it all. *All!*"

"What family secrets, Auntie? What are you talking about?"

"Never mind, honey. You don't need that kind of burden. You're better off not knowing. I wish I had never known."

Antoinette took a deep cleansing breath, and said, "But it's over for me. I've told it all to Bill, and he has enough to hold everyone who was arrested the other night... and more! And this time, they will be able to throw away the key!"

CHAPTER TWELVE
WINNER GETS IT ALL

Catarina brought out a large sheet cake with letters that read "THE INSIDERS" and a candy saw on top. The Insiders' laughter filled the library for the last time. And although the cake looked delicious, all they wanted to do was go home! Cat had large pieces of cake boxed up and carried out to the waiting limousines that she had ordered to deliver The Insiders to their homes, and stood on the front porch of the beautiful yellow inn. When the last limo disappeared down the driveway, Cat sighed and turned to walk up the four staircases to her Ivory Tower. Boy did she have a lot to write in her journal.

JIMMY—WHAT'S HE GONNA DO WHERE'S HE GONNA GO?

Although Ron drove Kat, Ronnie, and himself home in his own car, they were perhaps the happiest to finally be home. Their family had beat them there, and all were waiting inside.

Caroline and Angel had made a small buffet and Auntie brought a cake. Lenny and LJ were waiting on the deck shooting the breeze. Mrs. Capra was sitting in the rocking chair waiting to hold Baby Ronnie.

When the family had all gathered in the downstairs family room, Ron stood up and tapped his glass with a fork. "I think a speech is in order." Ron, who was usually uncomfortable making speeches, grinned.

"It's been said: 'All roads lead to Rome.' In

this case all roads—and bloodlines led to Jimmy Logan. And although his start in life was a sad one, and sure there were plenty of bumps and turns along the way, it's made him the strong young man he is today. A strong, *honorable,*—and okay, wealthy— young man, with the most honorable and intriguing plan imaginable. With the help of his dad, he's drawn up multiple business plans that will affect our community and beyond immensely! And in ways that touch everyone who has had a positive impact on his childhood—starting on Cobb Mountain with the expansion of Dr. Fleming's retreat and clinic, and reaching all the way to the Santa Cruz Mountains and Mare Vista, which Jimmy has signed over to Dr. Fleming. LJ's dad drew up plans long ago and is already in the makings for a long-term treatment center for depression and suicide prevention in memory and honor of Heather Logan." Ron gave pause as everyone seemed to appreciate a moment of silence for the brave young woman who endured so much sadness.

Continuing, Ron smiled at his young sister-in-law, "Angel will now have the funding she needs to see her plans for a horse and troubled youth' program to fruition. And although John Buchanan has generously pledged to partner with her on that with his trust fund, Jimmy has had papers drawn up to more than pick up the slack." This brought applause from those gathered together for this family meeting.

"And on another happy note, Mrs. Capra will be gathering all her foster boys and taking them on a cruise to Italy where *one certain foster kid* will finally be able to not only see but hike the volcano of

221

his dreams! Mount Vesuvius."

This brought a cheer from Little Jimmy, who knew of his plans for months, but couldn't share them.

"Children's Musem of Art and Science will also be receiving a gift of a new and improved volcano exhibit and butterfly exhibit, along with the pledge of operating funds being covered for the next... well... for a very long time.

"And as far as Mount Hannah goes—the plant will stop fracking immediately and, bottom-line set aside, research has begun on how best to move forward in the most ecologically and environmentally safe way and for the betterment of humanity.

"Oh, and more news. From what I understand, the once 'loner' PI, along with acquiring a life partner, is taking on a business partner. Someone who has already proved herself a *super-sleuth* and researcher. Kat has turned in her resignation to the county, and will add her name to Jack Moran's Private Detective shingle." Ron gave his wife a grin while adding, "She will *no longer* work in the field, but will restrict her work to research, which will be done on her home computer while raising our son."

Looking around, Bill Norris inquired about LJ's father, whom he would very much like to meet.

"Oh, you've met him, LJ grinned. And you liked him very much and he you. He's worked as a janitor in your office several times."

JOURNEY'S END EPILOGUE

Catarina and Eduardo Spidiacci delivered the following note to Ron and Kat Simmons, that was written by a W. T. Spears. It must have fallen from Sam's last journal, which was found later in the wall:

"My dad instructed me on his death bed to bring my family to California after my mother joined him in death. He told me of a journal his father hid along with other documents, on Cobb Mountain. His father had been disinherited because of marrying an Indian woman. But my father said he received a letter from Ireland saying he was next in line to inherit. I thought it was only the ramblings of a dying man. But years later, as my mother was saying her final goodbye, she told me the same story and told me to go claim my inheritance, and that everything I needed to know was hidden under a stone on Cobb Mountain and I could find a map in the wall of the stagecoach stop my grandfather built.

Still, it was only after receiving a letter from Ireland that I decided to make this trek—which led me dangerously close to being robbed at a river crossing on the way. We arrived late, and missed the last ferry, so had to camp. A lone cowboy showed up and sat on a rock, a stone's throw away, smoking all night. My wife sewed our money between her skirt and petticoat.

I built onto the stagecoach stop, adding more rooms and indoor plumbing and it eventually became Crossroads Inn Time Bed and Breakfast and Spa. To be clear, I made the trek, not to make claim to the

Irish estate, nor this inn. I'll admit to only being curious about my grandfather's journal. As for any inheritance concerning his Irish heritage—if anyone of my descendants are ever interested, I hope they will find this note along with the documents, and do what they might. As for me—if my dad wasn't good enough to inherit, then neither am I."

Ron looked into Kat's misty eyes and mused, "So the secret's been on Cobb Mountain, where the mystery began, all along." Kat's eyes widened as she exclaimed, "And it's still there!"

…the end

POST SCRIPT

Do you wonder about the outcome of Carolina Jane aka Celina McKenzie?

If you believe public bios, the famous Irish dancer led a wonderful life, she married had children and lived a long happy life.

However, what her bio left out was that, though she did finally get her inheritance, she chose to keep dancing, until she was wooed and won by a handsome dapper divorcee who showered her with attention and affection while wining and dining her down the aisle, at which time he promptly took over her money and life.

Yes, as her bio states she had children. Rather she gave birth to two daughters and a son, which her husband, with the help of the governess, who was also his mistress, raised into egotistical, selfish, manipulating images of himself. If the children showed any attention to their mother, it was with filled with disdain and disrespect.

Carolina, now a middle-aged widow of the tyrannical spendthrift, from an 'old established, but penniless family' that, though they never accepted her, welcomed her money which had supported them all the past three decades.

And yet Carolina Jane endured even that. To what end?

Do you worry about our poor little Carolina Jane aka Celina McKenzie, and wonder what was to become of her?

Well don't.

The little girl who watched her beloved mother die on the harbor dock, survived sleeping in the New York City ghettos and streets with her devoted young governess, danced her way into the hearts of many before getting lost from the wagon train west in the hot desert, fell off a cliff resulting in amnesia, then escaped her kidnappers by climbing up a hot chimney and joining an Irish dance troupe which took her all over America and Europe while trying to find her way back to her beloved Uncle Samuel Spears and Auntie Cat Dancer will not be brought down by a bad marriage.

We catch up with our heroine leaving her husband's funeral by way of the great lawn of her mother-in-law's estate.

Carolina Jane is walking, as per usual behind her mother in-law who is walking arm and arm with her former daughter in law—Carolina Jane's dead husband's first wife, followed close behind by hind by the adult children Carolina had given birth to. The 'family' is gushing with laughter and hushed

226

conversation meant to, and always seemed to succeed in causing Carolina to feel like an outsider. She was treated like baggage that was imposed upon them at holidays, and was looked down upon just as their father and his relatives had always done.

They had done their best to bury her celebrity status. The fact that she had danced before kings and was presented to Court was never spoken of. If her dancing career was spoken of it was referred to her making a shameful spectacle of herself *on stage*. Those last two words were always whispered.

On this day, however, Carolina unexpectedly mumbled something that brought everyone to a halt.

"What was that?" Her mother-in-law stammered in shock.

Carolina Jane wasn't whispering when she repeated herself to her dead husband's ex-wife:

"I am so glad I can count on you to take care of *her*, it means so much to me to know that she is taken care of; since I am leaving this evening for an extended holiday."

Walking briskly away, Carolina Jane catches a glance of the two allies standing with their mouths agape and arms at their side. Carolina couldn't hold back the wide grin spreading across her face, which took years off it and put a spring in her step as she all but danced toward the until now unnoticed new sports car.

The next family event took place several months later during the holidays; when Carolina Jane didn't show up, their back biting relief and laughter was

227

soon replaced with worry and concern for their hoped-for inheritance.

Their worry increased with the delivery of a telegram which read in part "We were having such a wonderful time in Greece that we couldn't bear to leave, perhaps we'll make it for Easter."

Carolina Jane's arrangement with the young unapologetic gigolo, Vince, was a 'never ending first date'. Although appearances spoke differently, the arrangement was all perfectly above board. Travel arrangements always included adjoining rooms. Caroline paid all expenses- even his ever-expanding wardrobe. But no cash was ever given. There was no sex, just good company, complete and adoring public attention and enlightened conversation. Only when Carolina suspected they were being observed did she allow a *hint of* romance.

When they were not together Vince was free to do as he pleased, but, on their dates and travels, there was no fooling around, not even the tiniest bit of flirting- nothing to demean her. She had quite enough of that during her long unhappy marriage!

Carolina had confided to a friend- yes, she actually had started having friends again- "All I want is good company, conversation, and a skilled dance partner. Oh yes, and a handsome young man to hang on to is more appealing than a cane, she laughed. All Vince wants from me is the experiences of travel, fine dining, fine clothes and maybe an inheritance-- but there's no promise." Taking a sip of champaign she added laughingly, "We might end up spending it *all* together!"

So, Carolina Jane aka Celina McKenzie spent the next decade or so traveling with her young escort, in between marching with fellow Woman's Suffrage leader Susan B. Anthony, until she became disillusioned with such an unfulfilling life. At which point she added the young Vince to her will and bid him a good and happy life.

Then one day while relaxing in her garden her lady's maid said there was someone at the door with a recording that she thought Carolina would be interested in. The message she heard changed her life and helped her see that real freedom and justice comes from an entirely different source and she spent the rest of her life knocking on doors carrying a similar record player.

So, you see, in the end the woman *does* get it all!

AUTHOR'S NOTE

Everyone has a story-- But not everyone has a good one.

My grandfather had a good one. He abdicated his inheritance, that of a 'house' of considerable size in Ireland, because his father was disinherited for marrying a Native American. Although my book is fiction, it was partly inspired by family folklore and stories my mother told. And when I was around ten, my grandfather, who was the most noble man I ever knew, received a letter telling him he was next in line to inherit. It was my grandfather's words I quoted: "If my father wasn't good enough to inherit then neither am I." I only wish I had a voice in the matter.

~Carolyn Jane (Kit) DeCanti